PROTECTED BY THE SPIDER'S WEB

ARIA WINTER
JADE WALTZ

Purple Fall
Publishing

Dedication

To my husband: Thank you for all your love and support. You are not just my husband, you are my best friend and my rock. I love you more than anything.

-Aria Winter

To My Husband,
Thank you for being my support and rock during this writing journey. I love you!

-Jade Waltz

CHAPTER 1

DAVIN

Kyra's been gone for several days, and the police have no idea what happened to her. She disappeared with some guy—Cael Renard—who owns the coffee shop down the block from our building.

According to the reports I've read, she'd only just met him. She went to his apartment that same day, and that was the last time anyone heard from them or saw them.

Cael's friend, Aris Pavone—co-owner of the coffeehouse —reported them missing after he found Cael's apartment thoroughly trashed later that day.

Closing my eyes, I picture Kyra's face. Her long blond hair, her gorgeous blue eyes and her brilliant smile. I imagine her sitting at her table in the coffeehouse, typing away on her computer as she writes her romance novels.

The police reports found no clear motive for the break-in or the disappearance, but I find it hard to believe it was just a random occurrence. From what I've learned, Kyra's apartment was broken into as well, which can't be a coincidence.

Someone was after them, but I don't know why or who it could be.

At first, I'd suspected Aris. He's the only one who connects to the two of them. After all, he's the guy who's been flirting with Kyra ever since she started going to that coffeehouse during the day to work on her romance novels. So, when I found out Kyra and Cael disappeared from his apartment, and Aris was the one who first reported it... I thought, for sure, he had something to do with it.

But now, I'm not so certain.

As I sit in front of my desk in my apartment, or what Poe refers to as my "command center," I'm glued to the left screen before me, watching as the detective—Seth Nathair—walks through Kyra's apartment for the third time. He picks up a few items, studying them curiously before setting them back down.

With his long, dark trench coat, short, white hair with green tips and pale green eyes I'm not sure what to make of this guy. He looks close to my age—mid to late twenties. But he dresses like a detective out of an old film noir or something.

He's meticulous about his job though, I'll give him that. He's combed through every centimeter of her apartment each time he's been there. He seems particularly obsessed with a snow globe for some reason, because he keeps going back to it with each visit.

His obsession with finding her rivals my own.

He sits down on the couch and runs his fingers roughly through his hair, sighing heavily in frustration.

"Where are you, Kyra?" he says. "What happened to you? Please, don't be dead."

My brow furrows. From what I've seen of his files, he's very dedicated to his job and he has a high rate of success in closing cases. I'm glad he's the one investigating her disappearance. Even at night, alone in his apartment, he goes through his evidence searching for more clues, hoping to find her.

From what I've gathered, he's married to his job. He doesn't do anything outside of work, sleep and eat. I can respect that. I'm the same way. We're loners, he and I. And it seems that each of us is obsessed with finding Kyra.

Funny thing is, he has a talking snake that lives with him, just like I have a talking spider. Turns out, we have a lot more in common than I thought. Who knew there were others out there who had *familiars* too? I'd figured I was the only one.

I thought it'd be more difficult to place hidden cameras at the police station and his apartment, but with Poe's help it wasn't as hard as I'd thought. When I planted the cameras in Aris's apartment, I did so believing that I would find some incriminating evidence linking him to her and Cael's disappearance.

I sigh heavily in frustration, because it seems I was wrong. Aris is just as worried as I am about his friend and the woman he's had his eye on for months. So, now I'm back to square one. With absolutely no idea what could have happened to them.

The detective has a blown-up image of Kyra's license picture on his wall, both at home and at work. It's clear he has other cases. His boss has gotten angry with him more than a few times when he's walked into his office and seen the image still on the display board. The soft glowing light of the screen scrolling through all the data he has gathered regarding their disappearance lit up the room.

He's dedicated, I'll give him that—almost as dedicated as I am.

I turn my attention to another screen and watch as Aris paces back and forth in his apartment, talking to his bird,

Fin, his peacock *familiar*. What are the odds the three of us would have familiars?

If there's anything I've learned in all my years as a hacker, it's that nothing happens by chance. Everything is connected in some way or another. You just have to follow the threads to figure it all out.

Everything is one big, interconnected web.

That's what I'm doing—following the threads until I piece together exactly what happened to Kyra and why I dream about her dying in my arms almost every night for the past five years.

I've hacked her and Cael's wristbands, but that turned out to be a dead end. I was shocked to see that there have been no charges and no travel as far as the data could tell. Aris, on the other hand, has gone back and forth between the coffeehouse, Cael's, and his apartment.

The building rumbles and the screens go dark as another earthquake disrupt the power for at least the twentieth time over the past week. I slam my fist down on the desk in frustration as I stare at the blank displays.

I clench my jaw when I notice my reflection. I haven't slept nor shaved in several days. My short white hair is sticking up from my head at odd angles, and my violet eyes appear dim from lack of sleep.

Poe comes up beside me. Her sharp gaze meets mine, and I'm struck by how human she can appear despite the fact she's a spider.

Well, not a spider in the typical sense.. She's purple and has six legs, two arms, and a head reminiscent of a bee with two large ovoid eyes and antennae. She blinks up at me with a pitying look, her crimson eyes searching mine.

"Do not get discouraged, Davin. If anyone can find her, it's you."

"I can't if nothing is working." Frustrated, I gesture to my now dead equipment and sigh heavily as I sit back in my chair. "What's with all these weird supposedly 'natural occurrences' anyway? The news just keeps dismissing the increased earthquakes, storms and tsunamis all over the world as 'acts of nature.'"

She gently pats my hand with one of her small front arms. "I'm sure you'll figure that out as well, with a little more digging."

"I just... I felt as though I was finally getting somewhere, you know? I mean, when I first saw her that day on the street several months ago, I knew she was the one from my recurring dreams. She's the woman who dies in my arms as I beg her forgiveness."

Tears sting my eyes, but I blink them back. "I love her, Poe. And that love tears my soul in two every night that I dream of her. It feels like a memory. But if it is, I don't understand how that could be. Part of me has always feared that it's a vision of the future. And now that she's gone, I feel like I failed her."

Poe's eyes meet mine. "You did not fail her, Davin. Do not be so hard on yourself. She is out there and we will find her."

I drop my head in my hands. "I miss everything about her, Poe, and we don't even really know each other."

Sadness fills me as I remember her music playing almost every night beneath my apartment. The way she bites her lower lip when she's concentrating, trying to figure out a plot point for her novel. How she always orders three bags of sour cream and onion chips each time she places her grocery order.

A smile curls my mouth as I think about how she, at first, tries to portion out a serving in a bowl, but eventually just caves and eats the rest of the bag in one sitting.

Closing my eyes, I draw in a deep breath as I remember

her scent—a combination of lavender and jasmine she mixes herself from essential oils.

My gaze drifts to the kitchen and the several boxes of those gourmet crackers I bought that she seems so fond of, as well as the cookies she always orders from France. She definitely has specific tastes in things. No one sells them around here, and she orders them special.

Now, I do as well.

As my eyes travel over my apartment, I realize just how far gone I am. Almost everything in here is the same as hers —soaps, towels, foods, even artwork.

I have every single framed poster hanging in my apartment that she does. In fact, they are placed exactly as they are on her walls.

I'm ashamed to say that I snuck into her apartment one day while she was gone. I took pictures of everything, wanting to decorate my place as she had hers. I don't know why, but doing this made me feel closer to her—as if we were sharing the same space. It was before I placed the cameras. Those didn't come until after she disappeared.

I've always been skilled at spying on people, but this was a step too far. I glance down at my desk and open the drawer that holds the matching pair of silk bra and panties I lifted from her laundry that day.

I fist the bra in my hand and bring it to my nose. Closing my eyes, I inhale deeply. When I open them, Poe is staring at me with a disapproving look.

"What are you doing?"

With a slight clench of my jaw, I lower my head.

"I don't know anymore."

CHAPTER 2

DAVIN

As soon as the power turns on again, I sigh in frustration when the cameras don't come back online in Cael's apartment. I'll have to go check them out and get them working again. A quick glance out the window and the dark clouds gathering above tell me that's not going to happen until tomorrow.

The weather has been so unpredictable lately. It's not unusual for what would appear to be a normal rainy day to suddenly turn into a tornado or a hail storm. I don't know what's going on with the planet lately, but something is wrong. I don't care how often the news insists everything is fine. It obviously isn't.

I sit back in my chair, and Poe jumps on my arm.

"You should go," she says. "You need to fix those cameras."

"Why is that?"

She tips her head to the side. "Because we both know you will not sleep, anyway. Not until you find her, at least."

Poe's right. I carefully place her back on the desk and

then stand. I sling my satchel over my shoulder and then pack my tablet and a few extra cameras in case the ones I already left at Cael's apartment were damaged beyond repair by the earthquake. I look at Poe.

"You want to come with me?"

"Yes." She smiles. "It would be lovely to get out for a bit."

I arch a brow. "You might not think that if the weather turns bad."

She shrugs. "Why should I worry? You'll keep me dry, won't you?"

"Of course, I will." I give her a mock bow. "I live only to serve."

She grins. It's a private joke between us. Since I met her, we've had an arrangement of sorts. She's a spider, yet... she's not. I thought since she looks similar to a spider that she'd do the typical "construct a web to trap bugs for food." But when I asked her about it, she stared at me, aghast.

She speak with a hint of a British accent, and appreciates the finer things in life—fancy cheese, bread, cucumber sandwiches and, of course, her daily tea with sugar and cream.

She loves to watch cooking videos, and we spend many hours in the kitchen recreating gourmet meals from scratch. When we're finished, I set her place at the table and serve her food and her tea on her tiny plate and small cup. I always make sure to do it with a flourish, as if I was her butler. It always makes her laugh, and I'm glad. Poe's not just my *familiar*, she's my best friend.

She hops up into my bag, and I note she has her tiny umbrella tucked under her arm. "What's that for?"

She tips up her head. "A lady never goes anywhere without proper preparation for inclement weather, Davin. You should know that by now."

"Oh." I laugh. "Forgive me, Lady Poe. I am but a mere peasant who often forgets these things."

"I shall overlook it." She gives me an imperious look and then grins. "This time."

It doesn't take long for us to reach Cael's apartment. As soon as we get there, I hack the door code to let us in. I don't bother to turn on the lights. Since I found Poe, I've developed the ability to see clearly in the dark. It's a handy ability to have. That and the fact that I can shoot webbing out of my fingertips and scale walls like a superhero.

Poe sits on my shoulder as I inspect the cameras. They are all still intact, but for some reason, they aren't sending out a signal. I pick up another one, trying to figure out the problem. It doesn't appear to be damaged, but—

"Someone's coming," Poe's voice is an urgent whisper. "We must hide."

My heart stops when I hear the click of the doorknob turning.

Gathering my gear and the cameras, I dash for the bedroom and slip inside the closet. Carefully, I slide the door closed behind me, leaving it open just enough so I can still see the room.

My eyes dart to the four-poster bed and the thick, green rumpled comforter and my nostrils flare. Kyra's scent still lingers in the place, telling me she was in this room. My gaze travels over the pale green walls and the several paintings of nature scenes, the desk and chair in one corner and the mirror opposite the bed.

Whatever happened, there was no sign of struggle in this room, but there is something strange about that full-length mirror. It has a slight glow around the edges, just barely visible with my enhanced sight. Poe noticed it when we were here before too.

When I touched it, flashes of my nightmare resurfaced, along with another image that I cannot let go.

Kyra and I were in a forest. She had tears in her eyes and I gathered her close. She reached up and cupped my cheek. "You and no other," she whispered.

I pressed my lips to hers, and whispered against them. "You and no other."

Poe jumps onto the door, pulling me back from my thoughts. She walks down the frame to peer out into the bedroom. She turns back to me, her red eyes easily visible in the darkness. "I'll find out who it is."

"No," I whisper. "Stay here. Someone might see you."

She tips up her chin. "I believe you are forgetting how stealthy I am."

"Poe, please listen to me for once," I plead. "I don't want you to get caught."

Pursing her lips, she gives me a pointed look and then proceeds to ignore me like she always does. She continues out the door. She moves along the wall and disappears around the corner.

The heavy sound of footsteps down the hallway fills me with worry. A bead of sweat trickles down my back as a light flicks on, the soft glow filtering into the bedroom.

Poe scurries back into the closet. "It's Aris and Fin—his peacock *familiar*," she whispers.

I grit my teeth. This complicates things. The last time Aris was here, he stayed for hours. I really don't like the idea of being trapped here for that long.

"I don't get it, Fin." His voice echoes down the hallway. "What could have happened? I should've been the one who took her home that day. Maybe if I had, they wouldn't be gone."

"You cannot blame yourself," his *familiar* answers. "You had no way of knowing something bad would happen."

As I listen to them talk back and forth, it's obvious he's in love with Kyra, and Cael is like a brother to him. He misses them both and blames himself for their disappearance. As much as I'm interested in their conversation, I'm even more interested in staying hidden and getting away. I don't want to get caught here. Not like this.

I look at Poe. "I think our best bet is to sneak out the window. What do you think?"

She nods.

Carefully, I slide the closet door open and tiptoe across the bedroom floor to the large window. Quietly, I prop it open and we slip out onto the fire escape. The metal clanks beneath my feet, and I cringe inwardly, worried it will draw Aris's attention.

I remain still a moment, but hear nothing.

I take great care to close the window without making a sound, and just as we start down the stairs, a flash of light catches my attention out of the corner of my eye.

I spin toward it and see Kyra, Cael, an orange cat and a white fox standing in the bedroom while Aris stares at them with a shocked expression that I'm certain mimics my own.

"What. The. Hell?"

"What is—" Poe starts to ask, then stops as she climbs on my shoulder and sees them too. "They're back!" she says happily. "Oh, this is wonderful, isn't it, Davin?"

My relief is short-lived. Dread settles deep in my gut as I observe Kyra with Cael. Aside from the fact they're dressed as if they just came from a medieval cosplay, the thing that truly bothers me more is the way he has his arm wrapped possessively around her.

What fresh hell is this?

CHAPTER 3

DAVIN

I watch through the window in shock. "Where did they come from?"

Poe shakes her head. "You saw them first. Did you not see them walk into the room?"

"No."

Sitting, I hide beneath the window as I pull out my tablet. I curse under my breath when I tap the display and find that my cameras still aren't working.

"What do you want to do?" Poe asks.

I run a hand roughly through my hair. I want to know where they've been and why they disappeared in the first place. Something isn't adding up. I meet Poe's red eyes. "Let's stay here and see what we can find out."

"All right." She nods and then settles on my knee.

A faint smile tips my lips. That's what I love about Poe. She may not approve of my spying on Kyra, but she understands my obsession in a way. She used to lecture me on why it would be a better idea not to observe someone without their knowledge. But after I explained my dreams of Kyra to her, she stopped.

As darkness settles on the city, I gaze out at the Sound. This guy has a hefty sum of money in his accounts and it shows. He has a prime view of the water from his bedroom. Seattle isn't an inexpensive place to live. As much digging as I did into his background, the best I could figure, the money was left to him as part of his parents' estate.

He lost both his parents in a transport accident, just as I did, but his loss was when he was a lot younger. There's another thing the four of us have in common. Me, him, Aris and Seth—the detective, are all without our parents. Judging by what I saw with the orange cat and the white fox, it seems each of us has *familiars* as well.

"What are you thinking, Davin?" Poe asks.

"All the strange coincidences between us. Each of us has a *familiar* and we're orphans, even Kyra. Her mom and sister died a few years ago. It's just... odd, don't you think?"

She shrugs. "You're the one who believes everything is somehow connected like a giant web. You just have to piece it together and follow the threads to understand how."

"That's true, Poe." I smile at her. "Sometimes I feel like you're the only one who understands me. The only one I can truly trust."

She tips her head to the side. "Do you ever wonder why I came to you?"

I shrug. "I used to, but you said you didn't know either."

Her eyes meet mine and she gives me a hesitant look. "Now that they've returned through the portal, there is something I must tell you."

I still. Whatever it is, I don't like the tone of her voice, nor the way she's staring at me with an expression somewhere between guilt and nervousness. "What is it?"

She places her front arm on my hand. "I did not come to

you by chance, Davin. You and I are connected. I was sent to you to help you find your queen."

"My... what?"

Her gaze shifts to the window.

"Kyra?" I ask, disbelief lacing my tone.

She nods. "You were meant to find her in this life."

I shake my head as confusion and betrayal fill me. "What are you saying? What have you been holding back from me?"

"Forgive me, Davin. There are things I could not and still cannot tell you."

"What do you mean?" I ask, my voice sharp with anger.

"I—"

She opens her mouth to reply, but a loud noise draws our attention back to the apartment. I spin to peek in the window, careful to keep my head down.

I frown when I see Cael with Kyra. He lays her on the bed and crawls over her. Anger boils inside me as he skates his hands up her thighs, lifting her dress. She gasps as he rips her panties from her body. My jaw drops when he dips his head between her legs.

I spin away from the window and toward the city, my back against the wall, clenching my jaw as I listen to the soft moans that escape her and the way she pants out his name.

He groans in pleasure, and I growl in frustration. Who the hell is this guy? And how is it that they're together after months and months of her being a semi-hermit?

He literally came from out of nowhere. In all the months I've been watching her, he never showed up until the day before her disappearance when he did that whole "knight in shining armor" thing, rescuing the cat from the busy street.

While I am not one who would ever want to see a creature suffer or get hurt, I sure did a lot of eye rolling that day as he practically ate up her adoration for his amazing and heroic feat of bravery.

What a loser.

He probably doesn't even know what her favorite ice cream is.

I do—white chocolate raspberry from a store around the corner. Her guilty pleasure every Friday without fail.

I've developed a taste for it myself. In fact, everything she loves, I've learned to love as well.

Except for Cael.

Sighing heavily, I sit forward and drop my head into my hands. I'll never like him. My hands curl into fists at my side as he groans again and she moans his name. When she begins declaring her undying love for this loser, each word from her lips is like a dagger to my heart.

Poe touches my arm. "Davin?"

"Don't," I hiss, turning my anger and frustration on her. "You act like you care, but you've been keeping secrets from me. Why?" I shake my head. "All these years we've been together… all these months you've watched me obsess over Kyra. And now you say that I was meant to find her?"

"I am sorry, Davin. Truly. But there are things I cannot tell you. Things you must discover for yourself."

I clench my jaw and look away from her. "How could you keep this from me, Poe? You know what I've been going through. I've told you about my dreams."

"I love you, Davin. You are my family. Please," she begs. "Forgive me. If I could tell you everything, I would."

"Why are you only telling me this now?" I ask incredulously. "You've seen how far down the rabbit hole I've fallen in my obsession with Kyra. Even *I* didn't understand it. Are you telling me now that you knew why this was happening to me? That there's a reason why I dream of her almost every night and a reason why my path crossed hers?"

She nods. "But it is something that I was supposed to allow you to discover for yourself, Davin. I still am."

"But, why? It doesn't make sense."

"I am bound by a power much greater than myself. One that spans time and worlds and destiny."

"So why are you telling me this now after all the months of silence?"

Her gaze sweeps back to the window. "Because I have long suspected that Aris was connected to all of this as well. And now, I believe, so is Cael." Her red eyes meet mine. "They were meant to find her too. Just like you were."

I grit my teeth as I think on all the months I've spent observing Kyra. Before Cael, the only person she ever had over to her apartment or interacted with on a regular basis, was her best friend, Claire.

Claire frustrated me to no end each time she tried to set Kyra up on a date. She even gave Kyra's number out to a few guys from her work, but I made certain Kyra never got their calls or their messages. I intercepted each and every one of them, sending them to their perfect match on one of those dating apps they didn't even know they signed up for.

They didn't know because *I* was the one who signed them up. Of course, they didn't question it when a line of beautiful women starting contacting them from these apps.

I even went as far as sending incentive payments to their matched women to string them along for a few dates, pretending to have a great time even if they weren't. I just needed these guys distracted long enough to forget about Kyra.

Do I feel guilty about it? Not in the slightest. Especially after I did some digging and saw how many women most of those guys have been through over the past few years.

Kyra is a romantic at heart. I've read all of her novels. Reading the words she has written is like having an intimate glimpse into her mind and her private thoughts. She wants... No, she *needs* a guy who will love her with all his heart and soul—a man who will place her above everything else in his life.

Someone like me. If she only knew how much I already love her, when we've barely said more than a few sentences to each other.

I turn to Poe. "What else can you tell me?"

She blinks up at me. "This may be difficult to believe but… she was your queen in a past life and you were her guard."

The image of her kissing me in the forest flits through my mind and I meet Poe's eyes evenly. "We were more than just queen and guard."

Although I say it as a statement, Poe understands it is also a question. She nods. "Yes."

I glance back at the window. "So, what was Cael to her? How do he and Aris fit into all of this?"

"Of that, I am uncertain," she says.

"What do you mean?"

"There are things that are still hidden from me as well. It is why I have not discouraged your… obsession. I am as desperate for answers as you are."

Even out here on the fire escape, I can detect Kyra's scent. It is much stronger now that she is being ravished by Cael and I can hardly bear knowing that he is even touching her.

She should be mine. Not his.

Sighing heavily, I drop my head back against the wall. I close my eyes and imagine running my fingers through the long silken strands of her hair. I long to taste her lips. How many times have I dreamed of making love to her?

I imagine rolling her beneath me. Her long, golden hair spread out beneath her on the pillow like a halo as she stares up at me through a half-lidded gaze. I would taste her lips and explore her mouth as my hands moved over her body. I would find that exact spot where she touches herself and cries out with pleasure.

I'm ashamed to say I watched her before when she has made herself come. I remember the first time I saw her. I was standing outside on the fire escape, observing her in the dark, through her bedroom window.

The light had been on, so she couldn't see me standing out there. My first inclination was to turn away and give her privacy, but with my newly developed senses, courtesy of Poe, the moment I scented her arousal, I couldn't move.

I stood there frozen in place and aching so badly with want to touch her. The purple lace bra and panties she had on are the ones I stole from her laundry right after she discarded them in the basket.

My heart pounds even as I remember that day. She never closes her curtains. They're always open, and I cannot resist the temptation to observe her. I know I should, but I'm too weak.

The sight of her pleasuring herself was better than any dreams I've conjured on my own of her.

Her soft cry draws my attention as she finds her release, and jealousy fills me. Apparently, this guy knows what he's doing because it's the same sound she has made when I've watched her come before.

Normally, all sorts of erotic images of me and her together would be filling my mind, but not now. Not when I know it's an actual lover who made her cry out like that instead of just herself and whatever she fantasizes about when she's alone.

I wish it was me. I wish I was the one with her in there now. Curling my hands into fists at my side, I struggle against the jealous rage that builds inside my chest. He'd better be good to her, because if he's not, I'll make his life a living hell.

I'll hack all his accounts again and drain every credit he has. I'll wipe his name and his record from existence, and he'll never be able to find a job.

"Are you all right?" Poe asks, concern easily heard in her tone.

I nod, but it's a lie. This is torture. I can't stand hearing her with another guy, not when I love her like I do.

Kyra deserves someone who will treasure and adore her like I do. The first time I officially met her in the elevator, it wasn't an accident. Kyra's a creature of habit, and I knew just when to intercept her for our first meeting.

I played it cool, acting as though I didn't know anything about her. In reality, I already knew everything. I'd even read all of her books. She is such a romantic at heart. I knew she'd want to be wooed, so I'd meant to take my time.

We'd have our first meeting in the elevator as if it were fate... and then maybe coffee and then some casual dating. All the while, making sure I did everything to make her fall for me.

I would buy her the pink roses she loves, and surprise her by meeting her for lunch at the café she writes in. We would go to the park and have romantic picnics and read together on the bench she loves so well. The one she likes because of the romantic dedication a man left for his wife on a small metal plate across the back.

I'd ask her to meet me in the overgrown area of the park and then sneak up behind her, wrapping my arms around her waist and pulling her back against my chest as I kiss a heated trail down the elegant curve of her neck. Just like in one of her romance novels.

I'd allow my hands to wander over her body with only the lightest of touches. Enough to awaken her desire but not enough to fulfill it—leaving her breathless and longing until she craves me as much as I crave her.

I'd planned when we made love the first time, it would be somewhere exotic and romantic, just like in one of her books. I'd take her slowly the first time. After that, I'd see if what she writes in some of her stories is what she's looking for.

Maybe I'd ask her if she'd like me to bind her wrists to the bed and give her pleasure until she's crying out my name and begging me to take her, like the heroine in three of her stories.

With a slight clench of my jaw, I listen as they make love again.

He'd better be good to her, I think to myself darkly. *Or else I'll make sure he pays for it dearly.*

I know one thing for sure. I'm not going to let her out of my sight again until I'm certain he's treating her well and treasuring her like the rare and beautiful woman she is.

This is the second day that Kyra has been back. The detective suspects, as I do, she wasn't on some exotic vacation. I know she wasn't. I saw her suddenly appear in her bedroom as if from thin air.

As I stare at the camera feed, I place another piece of popcorn on the desk for Poe. I just spoke with Kyra in the elevator. Her new boyfriend, Cael, is super possessive, but I already knew that from his body language when they first reappeared in his apartment. I shouldn't fault him. I probably would be too if she were with me.

The way he glared at me, I thought for sure he was going to say something when I winked at her, but he held back. I shouldn't have done it, but I wanted to get a rise out of him. I was hoping to send him spiraling into some uncontrolled rage, just so she could see that she needs someone else.

Someone not so dominatingly alpha. Someone like me, who would protect her and still allow her the freedom to speak with other men.

A short puff of air escapes me in frustration. Who am I kidding? I'd probably be just as bad at him.

Of course, if I was with her, she wouldn't even want to speak with other men. I'd fill her days with romance and her nights with so much pleasure she wouldn't be able to think of anyone else, much less even speak to them.

I'd fulfill every fantasy she has and find new ones she didn't even know she wanted. I open the drawer of my desk and pull out her lace bra. Bringing it to my nose, I inhale deeply of her delicate scent. I'd worship every centimeter of her body over and over.

She is mine, she just doesn't know it yet. But that will soon change.

Poe says we were together in a past life. I just need to find a way to make her remember. And once I do, hopefully she'll forget about Cael.

As I stare at the monitor, I shake my head as Cael's eyes flash with jealousy simply because his friend Aris is looking at her with the same kind of longing I feel for her. When Cael pulls her into the bedroom and pins her against the wall, my heart stutters then stops. Dread twists deep in my gut as he fumbles with his pants and then—

I shut down the display. Poe gives me a pitying look.

"I'm sorry, Davin."

"It's all right, Poe." I sigh as I lean back in my chair. "I'll get over it."

Even as the words leave my mouth, I know they're a lie.

A while later, just as I'm about to turn the cameras back on, loud sirens fill the air.

I dart a glance out the window and see three police trans-ports parked below, lights flashing. I flick the cameras back on and find Detective Seth Nathair staring at Cael warily as Cael explains Aris and Kyra fell madly in love with each other and left him.

"What the hell is going on now?" I drop the popcorn on the floor as I lean in, studying the screen as I turn up the volume to listen. "Did she really just disappear again?"

CHAPTER 4

KYRA

SEVERAL DAYS LATER...

I look at Cael and Aris. I hate that we have to leave already, but I know we must. Astra says the other guards are back on Earth and we have to find them.

My thoughts turn to Davin and his tall, lean muscular form. With his short-cropped white hair, handsome grin, violet eyes and a square jaw that could cut glass, there's something so familiar about him. He has to be part of Bryndon. Why else would I feel a pull to him?

Cael's teal eyes meet mine. "How are we going to locate this guy—Davin?"

Even though he understands we have to find the other guards, I don't miss the way the muscles in his jaw tick as he waits for me to answer. He has accepted Aris, but I don't know how easy it will be for him to accept the others once we find them.

I'd hoped knowing the others are all part of him—part of Bryndon—would help him with his jealousy, but it seems he's still struggling with his intense possessiveness.

"He lives in the apartment above me," I reply.

"That should make it easy," Aris says. His emerald eyes meet mine. "But now we have to figure out how to approach him about all of this."

"Perhaps simply by touch," Fin says. "Just as it was for you and Kyra."

"He's right," I offer. "Maybe if I touch him, it will trigger the memories as it did with both of you." I look at Cael and Aris.

Cael wraps a possessive arm around me and presses a tender kiss to my temple. I allow myself to melt in his embrace as he pulls me into a tight hug. His lean, muscular form feels so strong and solid around mine. I love when he holds me like this.

Tenderly, he cups my chin as he studies me like I'm a rare and precious treasure. "Then, let's go find him and see if he is, in fact, one of us. The sooner we find the rest of the guards, the better. I want you protected at all times."

I reach up and comb my hand through his straight, white hair. It's grown at bit since we were here last—hanging just below his brow. I brush it back as I study his handsome face and his teal eyes. With his aristocratic nose, cheeks and brow and his strong, muscular jaw, he is an exact copy of who he was before, when he was Bryndon in our past life.

Aris nods, and then turns his attention to the mirror. Astra stands beside him, her orange tail curled around her feet. Her green cat eyes observe him as he concentrates on opening a portal to Earth.

Aris is devastatingly handsome in his own right. It's so easy to lose myself in his gorgeous emerald eyes. With short chestnut hair and an angular jaw, he always projects such a quiet air of confidence around him. My gaze travels over his form. He and Cael are both tall, lean and muscular, but they are so different from each other.

It makes me wonder how the others will be once we find them.

Cael is fire and passion when we make love. Whereas Aris is gentle and slow, drawing out my pleasure with soft presses of his lips across my skin as he worships me like I'm some sort of goddess made manifest before him.

"I will take us all straight to your apartment, Kyra," he says.

"That sounds good."

"One thing I forgot to tell you before we go back," Cael interjects. "I told the detective you ran away together. That the two of you fell madly in love and left me behind."

I frown. "Why would you tell him that?"

"It was the only way to get him to leave me alone with all the questions about why you both had disappeared before he arrived to meet us at your apartment. I had to come up with a story on short notice."

I laugh, thinking what a terrible of a liar Cael is. "Your stories aren't very good, Cael. Just like when you told him we'd gone to Hawaii, of all places." I shake my head. "There's no way he actually believed that."

Cael shrugs. "He might have. You never know."

Aris rolls his eyes before returning his attention back to his task. Small sparks of energy crackle across the tips of his fingers as he raises his hands. Our image in the mirror ripples and distorts before fading away to reveal my bedroom in my apartment. I take Aris and Cael's hands and together we step through.

The world falls away and we're surrounded by darkness for a moment before we're suddenly standing in my bedroom.

As my gaze travels over the room, I'm struck by how both familiar yet foreign everything feels now that we've returned from the castle. The palace and the Otherworld feel more like home to me, and I find myself already wanting to return.

"You did wonderful, Aris," Astra tells him, drawing my attention back from my thoughts. "Your magic is very strong."

He smiles at the compliment. I squeeze his hand, then stretch up on my toes and give him a tender kiss. "You are amazing, my love."

I turn my eyes back to the room and the large four-poster bed. The sheets are tucked in, and the deep purple comforter and pillows are arranged as though it has been freshly made.

I turn and wrap my arms around Cael, hugging him close. "You cleaned up for me?"

"Of course. I was going crazy when you both disappeared, and the only thing I could do was try to keep myself busy." Tears brighten his eyes. "I was so worried for both of you. I…" He turns to Lynx and Fin and Astra. "If not for these guys, I would have been even more lost than I already was. They kept me sane, and convinced me to clean all of this up in anticipation of you returning." He darts a glance at Aris. "And now… we all have."

He sighs heavily. "I miss our home though in the castle."

"Me too," I agree.

Aris nods. "Now that more of my memories have returned, I feel a pull to return there and never leave."

I understand what they're saying because I feel this way too. Lunaria feels more like home than Earth does now.

"It has been such a long and arduous journey for us to return here." Lynx steps forward, his bright blue eyes staring up at us adoringly. He curls his fluffy white fox tail around his feet as he looks at Cael. "I believe perhaps some celebratory bacon may be in order, don't you?"

Cael rolls his eyes. "Any excuse for bacon," he mumbles.

I laugh as I look at Lynx. "You know you have an addiction, right?"

He blinks up at me with his cute little face. "I thought you were on my side. You promised to give me bacon whenever I needed it."

"You're right." I pet his head, and he leans into my hand. "I did."

"If he gets fat, it's your fault," Cael says, looking over his shoulder at his companion. "I've been trying to tell him he needs to cut back on the bacon. It's not healthy."

"I am not fat, I'm fluffy." Lynx growls and tips up his little fox nose. "Besides, I am beautiful, and you know it."

Fine," Cael tells him, then smiles. "Let's go a step further and order some pizza too."

A wide grin spread across Lynx's face. "That sounds wonderful."

Cael looks at Aris and me. "Maybe over dinner we can discuss searching for the others."

We both nod.

Cael leaves to place an order with Lynx trotting behind him, excitement evident in the swish of his fluffy tail.

Astra and Fin remain behind with me and Aris. Fin jumps up on the bed and settles down, his lovely blue-green and gold feathers tucked neatly behind him. His green eyes look up at us. "This is quite comfortable. I believe I will like it here."

Aris purses his lips. "Don't get too comfortable. You can't always be on the bed, you know. You might have to sleep on the couch."

He narrows his eyes. "Perhaps you should be the one on the couch, not me."

I laugh. "No one has to sleep on the couch. It's a king-size bed. Everyone should fit ."

Fin dips his chin toward me and his gaze darts to Aris. "At least someone here is making sense."

Aris rolls his eyes. "You're going to spoil him, you know," he teases me.

I run my hand over Fin's lovely feathers and grin. "A beautiful peacock like him should be spoiled."

Fin spreads his feathers wide and tips up his head, looking every bit as magnificent as he knows he is.

"And me?" Astra says, jumping up on the bed. Her green cat eyes blink up at me adoringly.

I smile. "You'll be spoiled too."

Walking into the kitchen, Lynx is on the counter, observing as Cael makes him a pan of bacon.

"I ordered the pizza," Cael says over his shoulder.

Aris and I take the lettuce and tomatoes out of the stasis unit and start making a salad to go with our pizza. I'm surprised at how well we all work around one another in the kitchen. It's as if we're in almost perfect sync as we get food ready and set the table for dinner.

I'd worried it might be crowded here in my apartment with the three of us and our familiars, but I'm pleased to know that I was wrong. Aris looks at me.

"We should probably only keep one apartment here on Earth, don't you think?"

I nod.

Cael glances over his shoulder. "Mine is the largest of the three, and it's fully paid off." His eyes meet mine. "Did you like it there?"

"Yes." His apartment was rather spacious compared to mine and it has a lovely view of the water. "Aris?" I look at him, wanting to make sure he agrees. I don't want to make any decisions that all of us aren't happy about.

"He's right," Aris replies. "His apartment is much larger than mine. It makes sense."

When the pizza arrives, we all sit around the table.

Dinner is wonderful. It's nice to relax for a bit after everything we've been through, but I know it can't last forever. We have things we need to do.

As if to remind me of our responsibility, the ground rumbles the building.

"Another one," Aris says. "They're getting more frequent."

A quick scan of the news earlier filled me with dread. Already the God of Destruction is causing havoc on this world. He and his followers have to be stopped.

"What are you going to do about that guy?" Cael asks, snapping me back from my thoughts, and I know he is talking about Davin.

Referring to him as "that guy" is not a good way to start. "If he *is* who we think he is, then he is a part of you, remember?" I point out.

With a slight clench of his jaw, he lowers his gaze. "I know. It's just... difficult," he admits. "At least with Aris, I know him." He smiles at his friend. "These others... I do not."

I take his hand and squeeze it gently. "I know. It's makes me a bit nervous too." I reach across with my other hands and take Aris's as well. "But together we'll figure this out. I know where he lives. So I think I'll see if he's home tomorrow and talk to him. See if anything clicks as it did for the three of us."

Cael nods, but the tense sent of his shoulders doesn't relax in the slightest. And part of me wonders, since each guard was part of Bryndon, will the rest of them feel the same possessive jealousy that Cael does as well?

Aris seems to not have as much difficulty as Cael, so maybe the rest of them won't either. I squeeze Cael's hand again.

He lifts his gaze to mine, pain visible behind his eyes. I would promise him I won't take the others as part of my

31

harem, but I cannot. He knows this. They were each part of him in our last life. How could I reject any of them knowing this now?

As if reading my mind, he leans in. "Forgive me. I will not repeat the mistakes of our past life. My vow."

"Neither will I," Aris adds. "We used to all be one. So now, we will embrace the others as our brothers."

My heart clenches at their selfless words. Even so... I can't imagine taking five men as my lovers. It's not something I ever thought I would do. My gaze drifts between Aris and Cael. I never thought I'd even have two men in my life like this, but here we are, and I wouldn't change anything about our relationships. I love them both. So much.

Aris looks between Cael and me "I think tomorrow we need to get things settled with the coffeehouse. We need to make sure it's looked after for our employees' sakes. Tara is a great manager, but we probably need to look into signing it over to her or something. Especially if the plan is to live in the Otherworld after this is all done."

"You're right," Cael adds. "We need to do that."

Aris turns to me. "Do you want to come with us?"

I shake my head. "No. I think I'll stay here."

"Before we go though, I think we should check out the guy from the elevator. See if he might be the third guard," Aris adds. "The sooner we find the others, the better."

Cael nods and gives Aris a knowing look. "You can read him then and see what you find out."

I just hope that if he is my third guard that he isn't the one who is destined to betray me.

When it's time to go to sleep, Lynx hops up on the bed and curls up next to my pillow. Cael grumbles as he carefully picks him up and moves him to the foot of the bed so he can slip beneath the covers beside me. Looping his arm over my waist, he pulls me back into the solid warmth of his chest.

The bed dips as Aris moves to my other side and he throws an arm over my waist as well. I snuggle between them as Lynx, Fin and Astra get settled near our feet.

I reach over Aris to shut off the light on the nightstand, but stop as he closes his mouth over my breast. I moan as he scrapes his teeth lightly over the sensitive peak through the fabric of my silken nightgown.

Arousal spikes through me. Aris loves to catch me off guard like this.

Warm hands snake up my thighs from behind as Cael pushes up my gown, dips his fingers under the band of my underwear and slides them down my hips.

Our familiars jump off the bed and leave the room, Lynx and Fin grumbling to themselves as they close the door behind them.

A low moan escapes me as my mates tease their tongues over my sensitive flesh. I doubt we'll get any sleep at all tonight.

CHAPTER 5

DAVIN

I blink in disbelief as Kyra, Cael, Aris, and their familiars all step out of the floor-length mirror in Kyra's bedroom. I had seen Cael and the familiars step through it and disappear only days ago, and I'd worried that they were gone for good, along with any chance of me ever seeing Kyra again.

I'm so glad she's alive. This is the second time she has disappeared and then mysteriously returned again.

Poe and I studied the mirror after Cael and the other stepped through a few days ago, but we couldn't get it to work. We tried to activate whatever portal they'd used to cross into what Poe says is the "Otherworld—Lunaria."

It's frustrating how my familiar and best friend will only give me tiny pieces of information about my past life but not enough to connect all the threads and understand everything that's going on.

Although I don't understand it, I push all my questions aside for now. Kyra is back, and that's all that matters.

"She has returned," Poe says, studying the screen.

"Yes, thank goodness." I breathe out a sigh of relief.

However, my relief is short-lived, when I watch her kiss both Cael and Aris. Poe turns to me.

"It appears as if she is mated to them both."

I grit my teeth. What the hell is going on here? Jealousy churns deep in my gut. She's supposed to be mine. Not theirs.

I turn up the volume, trying to hear what they're saying but the sound isn't working on my cameras. Aris kisses her long and deep as they work to prepare dinner together in the kitchen and I growl in frustration.

When Cael moves behind her and turns her head back to him for a kiss as well, I can hardly stand it.

I watch the cameras as they all have dinner together. When it's time for them to go to sleep, my heart sinks when they both get into bed with her.

Just when I think it could not possibly get worse, Aris takes her breast into his mouth as Cael removes her silken panties.

I quickly shut down the screen. I can't bear to watch her make love to another man, much less two. She's supposed to be mine.

Poe jumps on my arm and gives me a pitying look. "I am so sorry, Davin. I wish there was something I could do. I—"

"There's nothing you can do, Poe." I shake my head, pushing away from the desk. "Don't feel bad. I'll get over it. I have to."

With a heavy sigh, I run my hand through my hair and start for the kitchen.

"What are you doing?" she asks.

"Getting a bottle of wine," I call over my shoulder. "I'm going to need it tonight."

~

When morning comes, I squint against the sunlight coming in through the windows. My head pounds, and I groan as I sit up. Poe looks at me.

"How are you feeling?"

I swing my legs over the side of the bed and drop my head in my hands.

"Like I'm going to die," I barely manage to croak.

"A shower should help."

She's right. The few times I drank this much, a shower was an excellent remedy.

Making my way to the bathroom, I step under the warm stream of the shower and brace my hands on the wall as I bow my head, allowing the heat to seep into my skin.

My thoughts return to the image of Kyra in the arms of Cael and Aris. Unbidden tears slip down my cheeks, but the shower masks my pain well. I don't want Poe to know how devastated I am. She'll just try to cheer me up, and I don't want that right now. I'd prefer to wallow in my misery for a while just yet.

I've been studying Kyra for months now, dreaming of the day she'd be mine, but now... I know she never will be. She already has someone... *two someones, in fact*, I think to myself bitterly.

The doorbell chimes, and I hastily exit the shower, throw on a fresh pair of boxers and wrap a towel loosely around my hips to go answer the door.

It's probably my weekly grocery delivery. They usually come around this time in the morning.

Opening the door, my jaw drops when I see Kyra, Cael and Aris standing in the hallway.

Kyra's eyes widen as they travel over my form.

"Umm... I'm sorry," she says quickly. "I didn't mean to

37

interrupt your shower, and it's obvious we've come at a bad time, and—"

"It's all right," I reassure her. "I'm glad to see you. I've been worried."

"You have?"

It's hard to find words as she stands here before me. I want only to gather her in my arms and hold her close. I was so scared I'd never see her again—that I'd lost her forever.

To have her here now, I want to pull her to my chest and never let her go.

Her blue eyes study mine in confusion, and I realize I have not answered her.

Somehow, I manage to form words. "You've disappeared twice now." I cast a wary glance at the other two men, wondering why they're here. "And... I'm glad that you're back."

Her small brow furrows. "How did you know I was gone?"

I point to the floor. "No music lately. So, I figured..." My voice trails off. I can't tell her how I really know. She wouldn't understand.

"Oh, right." She smiles. "I'll bet you've slept well though without it lately, right?"

"Actually, no, I haven't." I shake my head as I stare deep into her lovely blue eyes. "I was worried about you, Kyra."

Cael narrows his eyes at me but Aris steps forward. He gives me a friendly smile and extends his hand in greeting.

"I'm Aris. I think we met briefly in the elevator."

I nod and take his hand. A strange warmth travels over my palm and a flurry of images flashes through my mind. Pressure builds at the back of my skull; the image of Kyra dying in my arms rushes through me.

Aris's emerald eyes stare deep into mine as if searching my very soul.

Unbearable pain fills me as my queen dies in my arms. "It was not you," Kyra whispers. "I know it was not you."

But as the dreams plays out in my mind, I know this is wrong. It was me. I was responsible for her death somehow, but I cannot remember why this is so.

Why would I kill the other half of my soul? The woman I loved more than my own life?

I cup her cheek and then gasp as red smears across her pale skin from my hand. I glance down at her mortal wound and notice the blood all around us.

I draw in a shaking breath. There's so much blood, and it's everywhere.

I press my hand to her injury, trying to stop the bleeding but it doesn't work. Her breaths are shallow and ragged as her blue eyes stare up into mine.

Panic beats at my chest as her eyelids flutter open and closed as she struggles against the death that will claim her.

I did this. But why?

Her eyes close and she goes still in my arms. I gather her to my chest as a feral roar of anguish rips from my throat.

"Davin?" Kyra's fingers touch my cheek, pulling me from the nightmare. "Davin, what's wrong?"

The world tilts and spins all around me. Unable to remain upright, I fall back onto the floor.

Kyra drops to her knees before me, and I reach up to cup her face.

"Forgive me," I breathe. "Forgive me, my queen."

CHAPTER 6

KYRA

I watch in horror as Davin's eyes roll up in the back of his head and he falls back. I drop to my knees. "Davin!"

His violet eyes meet mine as he reaches up to cup my cheek.

"Forgive me," he rasps. "Forgive me, my queen."

Cael and Aris hover over him.

"What happened to him?" Cael snaps.

"I—I don't know," Aris answers. "I was trying to search his mind, but something went wrong."

I look at them. "Help me get him to the couch."

They pick him up, and we move into his apartment, carefully placing him on the sofa.

Kneeling beside him, I brush the hair back from his forehead.

"Davin? Please wake up," I plead.

"What happened to him?" a small voice calls out.

I whip my head toward the sound and notice a small spider-looking creature on the desk in the corner of the living room. I blink several times as my eyes travel over her form.

She's a little bigger than a regular spider, but her body is strange. She stands on six legs and uses the front two as arms as she gestures to Davin on the couch. She lifts her ovoid head to me as her two antennae move back and forth. Her red eyes meet mine. "Is he all right?"

"Wha—who are you?" I ask.

She tips up her chin. "I am his familiar. Now, tell me what happened to him," she demands.

"We don't know," Cael answers.

Aris moves toward her. "You are his familiar?"

"Yes, my name is Poe."

"I'm—" he starts, but she continues.

"You are Aris and you are Cael." She looks at Cael and then her gaze sweeps to me. "And you are Kyra."

"How did you—" I start to ask but stop as my eyes scan the room. I stare in shock at the walls, noting that Davin has the exact same artwork as I do, and it's placed in the same positions. I look toward the kitchen and notice a box of the same gourmet crackers I order each week with my grocery delivery. They're sitting next to the Parisian cookies I special order from the international market as well.

The dish towel hanging from the stove is purple with tiny white roses like mine and as my gaze travels over the sink I note he even has the same brand of lavender soap I use.

Poe starts toward me, front arms raised as if in a placating gesture. "I know this probably seems strange to you, but—"

"Why does this look exactly like what I have in my apartment?" I gesture to the walls, the artwork and the kitchen.

Cael's and Aris' expressions darken as they notice it too.

"And the same foods that I special order?" I gesture to the counter. "Why does—"

Poe shakes her head. "I know this looks bad to you, but it's not what it seems. I swear."

"Really?" Cael asks, his voice thunderous. "Because it looks like Davin is a stalker."

"He's a good man," she says. "He is just… complicated. He means no harm." She walks over the keyboard and the five monitors suspended above his desk flick on.

Shock, quickly followed by anger, fills me when I see the interior of my apartment, including my bedroom, on one of the screens.

"That's Aris' apartment, yours, and mine," Cael growls as he stalks toward it. "And that,"—he points to the display—"is the detective at his office."

A tablet on the table flickers to life, and I stare in stunned silence at the image frozen on the screen. It's of me, Cael, and Aris lying in bed together.

Davin groans and lifts his head. "What happened?"

"What is this?" I shove the tablet in his face. "Why have you been spying on us?"

His eyes go wide, and he reaches for the display. The moment his hands touch the screen, the world falls away and we're spiraling through darkness.

CHAPTER 7

DAVIN

Kyra and I tumble through a darkened void. As we flail through pitch-black nothingness, my first instinct is to protect her. I reach for her, wrapping myself around her smaller form.

I blink and my back slams to the ground, forcing the air from my lungs as Kyra's weight crushes against me too. Unable to move, I stare up through a jungle of thick vegetation and trees overhead. I draw in a shaking breath as my mind struggles to reconcile the fact that we're no longer in my apartment. We're... somewhere else entirely.

Kyra rolls off my chest. With a pained groan, I twist onto my side. I allow my gaze to travel over her, searching for any sign that she is injured. "Are you all right?" I ask as I reach for her.

She jerks away as if my touch were fire, fear evident in her eyes as they meet mine. "Don't touch me," she snaps.

I drop my hand back down to my side, giving her space.

She stands, and I do too as she gives me a wary look.

I raise my hands out before me in a placating gesture. "Look, I'm not going to hurt you. I swear." I turn my gaze to the surrounding jungle. "Right now, we need to figure out where we are, all right?"

"I already know where we are." She glares at me. "We're in Lunaria—the Otherworld."

"The... what?" I ask as I scan the area.

I remember Poe mentioning this place. She said it's where I lived in my previous life. She didn't give me much detail beyond that and now I wished I'd pressed harder for more information.

The ground is spongy beneath my feet and covered with a layer of purple moss. A thick forest surrounds us. The trees are heavily laden with glowing violet leaves, their trunks covered in the same moss that blankets the soil. Long green vines wind tightly over many of the branches and then spill down to the ground, swaying in the breeze like living curtains. The vegetation is so dense it blocks out most of the light from the sun, and only small patches of light blue sky are visible overhead.

"Lunaria," she says again. "The Otherworld. That's where we are." She cocks her head to the side. "Does any of this seem familiar to you in any way?"

My brow furrows, wisps of broken memory flit through my mind and I nod.

"It's like... a dream... an image or vision. It's like a memory but... not. It's fragmented, in a way."

"Do you remember anything else?" she asks, irritation evident in her tone.

She narrows her eyes, and I recall her shoving my tablet in my face—the image of her asleep with Cael and Aris displayed across the screen.

"Kyra, I—I'm sorry about the cameras. I was—"

"Spying on me?" she snaps. "Is that what you were going to say?"

I swallow thickly. What can I say to that? It's true.

A thought occurs to me.

"Why are you not more concerned that we're in a forest with purple trees and moss? Have you been here before?"

She nods.

Understanding dawns. "Is this where you came from when I saw you step through from the mirror?"

Her eyes flash with anger. "Yes," she replies darkly. "But I'm guessing that's not all you saw, *is it*, Davin?"

I run a hand roughly through my hair. "I can explain. Please, let me—" I stop as a strange noise draws my attention.

"What is it?" she asks, alarm in her features.

"Something is coming." Although I don't know what it is, whatever approaches fills me with dread and fear. As if I can somehow sense it is evil. "We need to hide."

We move behind a large tangle of roots beneath a nearby tree. My nostrils flare. The forest around us is earthy and damp, but a strange scent carries on the breeze. Thick and cloying, it grows stronger. A smell that instinctively makes my heart race with a mixture of fear and anxiety. I peer through a small opening in the thick mass of roots and moss, waiting in silence to see what it is.

"I know you are here," a dark voice whispers through the woods.

My sharp eyes scan the forest, but I see no one nearby.

"You can try to hide, but it is no use. Her light is so strong it cannot be hidden from me."

A wisp of black smoke curls up and over the roots, spilling to the ground like water into a dark pool near our feet.

I wrap my hand around Kyra's forearm and pull her behind me as a dark hooded-figure rises up from the smoke.

Glowing red eyes stare at us from an inhumanly pale face. The small amount of light affords me a view of his harsh and angular features. The man standing before me as much human as he is a dark and twisted creature.

Memories flood my mind and I realize this man is not merely a Dark Mage. He is a Guardian of Destruction.

Panic beats at my chest as he reaches a skeletal hand towards Kyra.

Images of a life that was mine resurface as I look to her. She was Alora. My queen is a Guardian of Creation. I am her guard and I must protect her, no matter the cost to myself.

This newly remembered knowledge stokes flames of anger and rage deep within. As long as I draw breath, the enemy will not touch her. Without hesitation, I lift my hand and shoot a string of webbing from the tips of my fingers, binding him tightly.

He drops to the ground like a stone and then begins writhing against the webbed netting.

I glance at my hand; I had not remembered until now that I could do this. Energy crackles across the tips of my fingers and I turn my attention again this foe.

In his gaze my feral reflection stares back at me, fierce and monstrous to behold. My eyes are now pitch-black orbs; dark fangs extend on either side of my mouth as I bare them, growling low in my throat.

"You think this will hold me?" he seethes.

Glowing red light surrounds him, melting the webbing away.

Kyra moves to my side, a glowing blue flame hovering above her palms. With a sharp flick of her wrists, she sends the fire spiraling toward him.

He cries out as it slams against his cloak in a fiery explosion, throwing him back to the ground and engulfing him completely.

"We have to run!" She grips my wrist and pulls me with her.

We race through the jungle. The vegetation is thick, but she pushes it aside as I follow behind her, crashing through the leaves and leaping over the thick tangle of roots of the trees that surround us.

A red flame rushes past us, exploding on the tree trunk up ahead.

I spin to find our attacker only a few steps behind us and closing fast.

My heart hammers. There's no way we'll outrun him.

"Join us or die!" he cries out.

Anger floods my veins and burns through my body like acid. Something dark and primal rises within me, and I give myself over, surrendering to its power and hunger.

"Keep running, Kyra!"

Dark and predatory instincts fill my mind as I face him. Venom drips from my fangs as my nails extend into sharpened, black claws.

"Davin, what are you doing?" she calls, but I dare not turn back.

Lightning fast, I leap toward him, sinking my teeth deep into his neck.

An inhuman shriek fills the air as he struggles to break free of my hold. "It burns!"

I retract my fangs and watch as he falls to the ground. Twisting and writhing, he wraps his hands over the injury. Angry black veins creep across his skin from the twin puncture wounds, spreading across his face and arms. His eyes are wide as he opens his mouth to speak, but only a choked gurgle escapes him along with thick foam, tinged pink with his blood.

He claws at his neck, struggling to breathe, and then goes still. I watch in satisfaction as the light fades from his eyes.

When I turn to Kyra, she inhales sharply and conjures another ball of blue flame in her hands.

"Stay back!"

I blink in confusion.

In her gaze, I see my reflection—my eyes are feral, obsidian orbs, two long fangs extend from my upper canines, and my skin is a deep purple hue.

I glance down at my hand, turning my palm over as I study it. I will my black claws and fangs to retract, watching in wonder as my skin returns to its normal tone.

"What the—"

Even as the question starts to leave my mouth, memories flood my mind, and I lift my eyes to Kyra. "I remember now," I breathe.

Flashes of images of her lying so trustingly in my arms after we'd made love. Not in this life, but in our last. We were more than guard and queen. She was my beloved.

Sadness fills me at the memory of my beloved queen dying in my arms. I drop to my knees before Kyra.

"Alora." My voice quavers. "Forgive me, my beloved queen."

A featherlight touch on the top of my head draws my attention up to her. Her eyes are filled with tears.

"Are you really him?" she asks softly.

I stand and gently reach for her face, the tips of my fingers hovering just above her cheek. In her gaze, I see I've returned to my regular form, but her eyes still shine with wariness. She does not trust me.

"It's me… Bryndon, my beloved. Do you not remember?"

With a slight clench of her jaw, she nods.

I step toward her, but she moves back and away from me.

"Why were you spying on me?"

"I—"

A nearby chorus of voices sounds in the distance. I meet her gaze evenly.

"I vow that I will not harm you, my queen. But we must leave here before we are discovered."

She nods, and together, we race further into the forest.

We keep running until we're both out of breath. Panting heavily, we stop and struggle to listen for anything behind us. Trying to determine if anyone has followed our trail.

"Do you think we lost them?"

I train my ears toward the direction we came from. Closing my eyes, I focus on the sounds of the jungle. Insects trill in the thick vegetation while strange animal cries fill the air.

"I hear nothing to indicate they are nearby."

I lift my gaze to the trees all around us. The sky is darker now, and it seems night may soon be approaching. "I think we should shelter here."

Her small brow furrows. "Where?"

I glance down at my open palm. "Leave that to me."

Memories fill my mind and I remember what to do. Lifting my hands, I cast out strings of webbing from the tips of my fingers. The thick and silken threads adhere to the trees overhead as I string lines back and forth between them, creating a web.

I make sure to reinforce the threads and wrap the supporting lines around the thick trunks and branches for extra security. I do not want to risk overlooking any potential weakness in the structure. It will need to hold our weight without issue.

Kyra stands beside me, gaping as she observes.

When I finish, I step onto the outer ring of threads, testing their strength. Satisfied they are more than strong enough for the two of us, I turn to her.

"The tension along the lines will alert us to any movement if someone or something tries to approach."

"But where will we sleep?" she asks, staring at the webbed configuration in wonder.

I grin and raise my hands again. "Leave that to me."

CHAPTER 8

KYRA

I watch with awestruck wonder as Davin creates a human-sized web among the trees. Memories return as I recall him doing this in his spider form. As terrifying as his shifted appearance was at first, I am not frightened now.

Bryndon took this form many times. He was lethal in this form, and while my memories make me inclined to trust him, I don't know what Aris saw in his mind. I didn't have a chance to ask him before Davin and I were transported to this world.

As I watch him create a cocoon-like bedding area for us to rest, I can't help but wonder if this is all an elaborate trap? He saved me earlier, but what if he's the one who will betray me? What if whatever caused Bryndon's madness in our last life has infected his mind now and is only waiting to be activated by the Dark Mages and the Guardians of Destruction?

He turns to me, smiling as he gestures to the silken,

tightly threaded area. It reminds me a bit of a hammock in the middle of all this webbing, but large enough for two.

"We can sleep there."

"*We* aren't sleeping anywhere," I tell him. "You need to make two of those. I'll sleep on one, and you can sleep on the other."

His expression falls. I expect him to protest, but he nods and begins to spin another bed.

When he's finished, he reaches his hand to help me walk the tightrope-like threads, but I pull away. I don't entirely trust him yet, and I would rather have both hands free in case I need to conjure my fire to defend myself from him.

He steps back, balancing on the thread as if it were completely effortless for him. Which... I suppose that it is.

I extend my arms out to my sides for balance as I walk on one of the outer rings. Breathing in and out through pursed lips, I focus on maintaining my balance. Slowly, I ascend each rung of the web toward the center, going higher and higher from the ground with each step.

I'm so far up now, a fall would be devastating to say the least. I'm glad the webbing is so tightly knit together. If I do happen to fall, I should be able to grab onto the nearest thread and pull myself back up.

Davin watches in silence, standing nearby, I suspect, to catch me if I should lose my footing.

"I can help you, Kyra," he offers in a soft voice.

"No, thank you," I reply tartly. "I prefer you to watch. You're good at that," I add, bitterness tinging my voice.

He sighs. "Please, Kyra. Let me explain."

Sweat trickles down my spine as I continue on.

"What is there to explain, Davin? You were spying on me, watching me and my mates without my consent," I grind out. "How long?"

When he doesn't answer, I chance a glance at him. His expression is full of guilt as his violet eyes meet mine.

"Months," he finally answers. "Ever since I bumped into you on the street."

I blink at him.

"I've been dreaming about you for years. The image of you—" His voice catches before he continues. "Dying in my arms, Alora. One day, you passed me, and we accidentally bumped into each other. You—" A slight grin tilts his lips. "You spilled boiling hot coffee all over my shirt."

As I study him, the memory flits through my mind.

"That was over six months ago." I frown. "Are you telling me that you've been watching me ever since that day?"

His violet gaze holds mine a moment before he answers. "Yes. In that moment, I knew you were her—the woman from my dreams. Only... now that my memories are returning, I know you don't look like Alora, even though I know you are her."

I frown as I consider his words. Strangely, in the dream, he saw me in this form instead of how I was in our last life. I wonder if it will be this way with the others.

"I think fate wanted me to find you. That's why I dreamed of you as you are now," he says, and I wonder if he has somehow read my thoughts.

His eyes search mine. "Do you remember what we... were to each other before?"

A thunderous roar fills the air, startling me, and I fall forward. Panicked, I reach for the closest thread. The tips of my fingers graze the silken line as I miss. A terror filled cry rips from my throat as I begin spiraling toward the forest floor.

In a blur of motion, a string of webbing surrounds and wraps tightly around my entire form, halting my descent.

With my arms and legs bound by the silken fibers, Davin begins to pull me back up.

At first, I'm afraid. With my hand at my sides, I cannot conjure a flame if I need it. I'm completely at his mercy. If he means me any harm, there is nothing I can do to stop him now.

As he hauls me up, I lift my gaze to his and he flashes a devastatingly handsome smile.

A memory returns of him binding me like this, sending a spike of arousal straight through me. It used to be something we'd do when he shifted into this form.

As if somehow sensing my thoughts, he stops, and I slowly spin, still caught in his web. When his violet eyes meet mine, full of desire, heat scalds my cheeks.

His nostrils flare as his hungry gaze travels over my form.

"Your scent," he rasps. "I remember that we—"

"Unbind me," I command, not wanting to admit to recalling these erotic memories. Besides… I still don't know if I can trust him.

He gathers me in his arms, then partially shifts. His nails extend into sharp claws, and he carefully slices the tight threads from my body. He's still holding me. His violet eyes stare deep into mine and a memory of us in our former life surfaces in my thoughts.

"I would never hurt you, Kyra," he whispers. "I only want to protect you, my queen."

His expression is so sincere it nearly breaks me. I want so badly to believe him. Emotions lodge in my throat and I cannot speak.

He carries me to the first bed and gently sets me down. The threads are as soft as silken fibers as I lie back on them. His gaze holds mine a moment before he turns away and moves to the separate bed nearby.

I turn my attention to the night sky, staring up at the stars that at once seemed so foreign but are now familiar instead.

"I shouldn't have been watching you," he speaks softly. "I know it was wrong, but I... needed to understand why I dreamed of you for so long. At first, it was a search for answers, but then..."

"Then, what?" I press.

"I fell in love with you."

"You don't know me," I protest. "We've barely even spoken to each other."

"I *do* know you."

I narrow my eyes. "I suppose with all your spying you probably think you do."

"You were Bryndon and I was Alora. I remember this now. I know we were more than just queen and guard. Do you—"

I cut him off. "Just because we were lovers in our past life doesn't mean we automatically are now. I don't know you, Davin. All I know of you in this life is that you spied on me. For months without my knowing."

"Please, my queen, forgive me."

I turn to him, his violet eyes glowing softly in the darkness as he watches me intently. "How much did you see, Davin?"

"I could not bear to watch you with them, if that is what you are asking," he answers, having guessed my question. He lowers his gaze. "Do you remember me? Do you remember everything that we were to each other?"

I understand he is asking this because he does not know that Aris and Cael are part of him—part of who he was. I'm not sure how to explain, but I know I must try.

"I remember, Bryndon, I..."

A cold breeze rushes over us, and I shiver slightly. He moves to my side with a stealth and speed I'd not thought he would be capable of. But then again, he is able to partially shift into a spider. "If you will allow me to—"

I shrink back, not wanting to be too close to him.

"Why are you afraid of me?" Sadness steals over his features. "Do you believe I watched you all that time because I wanted to hurt you?" He shakes his head. "I watched you because I wanted to know more about you and to protect you."

"Protect me?"

He looks down at his hands. "Something inside me wanted to protect you, to watch over you and make certain no harm could ever—" His voice catches. "I know now why I did it, but I didn't understand it then. As your guard... even before we were lovers, you were always first and foremost on my mind.

"The need to be near and protect you was almost maddening in its intensity. I would check on you several times during the night as you slept." He pauses. "I was good at watching you from afar, but making certain I was close enough I could keep you from danger."

Understanding dawns. "You purposefully moved into the apartment above me, didn't you?"

"After that first day I saw you, I followed you, Kyra. I found out where you lived and I... offered the guy above you twice what the apartment was worth so I could move in, and then..." his voice trails off.

"And then what? You placed the hidden cameras?"

"No. I didn't place those until you disappeared. I was desperate to find out what happened to you... searching for any clues. I was trying to keep up with what the detective was doing for your case as well. Sometimes, I think he was as obsessed as I was with finding you."

"Why do you say that?" My curiosity is piqued.

He gives me a guilty look before he answers.

"Because the cameras I placed in his apartment... I watched him go over your case every night, searching for clues. He fell asleep so many times with your file open on his tablet."

Maybe Cael and Aris's suspicions are right, and perhaps the detective might be one of my other guards. I felt a pull to him when we spoke.

The cool air rushes over me again, and I cross my arms over my chest, desperate to warm myself however I can.

"Please," Davin says. "Let me hold you. I promise I won't do anything you do not wish."

I study him a moment, deciding. As much as I want to trust him... I just can't. Not yet.

He raises his hands and begins weaving a tightly threaded web so thick, it takes me a moment to realize it's a blanket. He hands it to me.

"Use this. It will help keep you warm."

I give him a faint smile. "Thank you."

I tug the web blanket over me and lie down. I'm tired, but my mind keeps going over the warning High Mage Talwyn gave me and Aris—one of the final three guards will betray me, but we don't know who.

Aris tried to read Davin, but something went wrong. Part of me wonders if maybe it was a safety placed in his mind by the Dark Mages, a way to keep his thoughts from being discovered.

There is also a risk that he may be like Bryndon was. Bryndon did not realize, until it was too late, that his mind had been manipulated by the Dark Mage who betrayed him.

I turn onto my back, making certain I can still see Davin out of the corner of my eye while I stare up at the stars.

He lies down in the bed beside mine.

A memory of our life before, flits through my mind.

I turn onto my side and nestled in his arms as he holds me close his chest. He presses a tender kiss to my lips and then traces them with the tip of his finger. His eyes traveling over me like a gentle caress—as if memorizing the contours of my face.

"I've loved you from the moment we met," he whispers. "One look in your eyes, and I knew my heart no longer belonged to me. It was yours, Alora. You and no other."

"You and no other, my love," I smile against his lips. "You are mine, and I am yours."

"I remember this," he says, pulling me back from the memory. "We used to lie in my web and look up at the night sky after we'd—"

"After we'd made love," I finish. A wistful smile crests my lips. "I remember the time it was so cold, you made this cocoon-like bed that completely encapsulated us."

"We were so tired and breathless after the second round, the cocoon was like a furnace inside." He grins. "I had to open up part of it because you complained you were too warm."

"Do you remember anything else? About our lives from before?"

"Many things are returning to me."

"Like what?"

He lifts his gaze to the tree canopy overhead.

"This place is Linzyra—the western province. We came here shortly after I became your guard. I transformed, and you held onto me as we swung through the trees with my webbing."

"That was such a fun day, but my mother didn't think so."

He arches a brow. "I wouldn't normally have been so bold but you were—"

I laugh. "Oh my gosh, I remember… I went into the forest with Prince Kinys, and he tried to kiss me. And that's when you showed up out of nowhere, and ripped me from the ground and started swinging through the trees." I narrow my eyes. "Were you jealous? Even then?"

He nods. "I could not help it. I was already in love with you."

Heat warms my cheeks. "I remember how you bound me to the tree with your webbing as a joke and then—"

"I leaned in and nearly kissed you." He finishes my sentence. "I wanted to... so badly."

Tears sting my eyes. "I wish you had."

"Why?"

"Because then we would have had more time together, Bryndon. Instead, you wasted those years just watching over me."

He shakes his head. "They were not wasted, Alora. I... think that's why I watch you now. Why I am obsessed with you. Why I cannot allow you to go anywhere without my knowing where and who with. As your guard, I used to track your every move as if I were you shadow. When you disappeared with Cael and then with Aris, it nearly drove me mad."

As he speaks, I understand that part of the reason he watched me so intently is because it was what he did when he was Bryndon. This is the part of him that is now in Davin. He was obsessed with protecting and watching over me. I can forgive him for his spying now, but I... still don't know if I can trust him.

"And now that you have taken two lovers, I—" He pauses, tears brighten his eyes, but he blinks them back. "I can hardly bear it."

He clenches his jaw and looks away. "I'm sorry. That's how I feel and I know I have no right. I never had any right. I was only ever supposed to guard you. To be your loyal servant and nothing more. I did not deserve you or your love, my queen. And I will not pretend that I believe I am deserving of it even now."

"Davin, you don't understand. They are—"

"I heard you, Kyra." His voice quavers. "I heard your passionate cries, and I knew they were real, and it kills me." He pauses. "Forgive me. I know this is a different life. A new one. What we were before has no bearing on what we are to one another now."

"But it does, Davin.,"

"What do you mean?"

"I was destined to be mated to five men. To take a harem in my last life, but I didn't because I fell in love with you. I only wanted you."

"That is who they are?" He cocks his head to the side. "They are your harem that you were supposed to have taken?"

"Yes, but there's more."

"I am destined to take five, even in this life, but it's not what you think. It's—"

Something tugs at the web, and his head jerks up. He stills, his violet eyes blinking in the darkness.

"What is it?" I whisper.

"Something approaches."

Stealthily, he moves along the webbing, making certain not to disturb it. I wait in silence, my heart hammering as I listen for any sounds, but all I can hear is my own pulse pounding in my ears.

After a moment, I hear him call out.

"It is all right. It was simply an animal passing through."

"Are you sure?" I ask, trying to keep my voice low.

"Yes. I can scent him. We are safe, Kyra."

I blink and then gasp as I look up and find him hovering over me, spinning slowly as he hangs by a thread from a branch above.

"Sleep," he soothes. "I will keep watch along the edges of our web. Tomorrow, we will figure out exactly where we are and what we need to do to get home."

My mouth is still gaping as I stare up at him, but I quickly snap it shut. I nod, but I'm pretty sure I'm not going to get any sleep, especially not with how fast and quiet he can move. If he is the one who will betray me, I'm in trouble. He's fast, quiet and lethal.

Even though Cael and Aris can shift forms, I never felt fearful of them. But it's different with Davin.

I think about his fangs in his partially shifted form. His venom worked quickly to end the life of the Guardian of Destruction. Davin didn't ask me about him. He didn't ask me to explain what he was or why he was after me.

He hasn't asked me anything about this world or our previous life, save for how much I remember about us—our relationship. And I'm not sure how much I should tell him.

So, either his memories have returned much faster than Cael and Aris's did, or he's already come to this world before, in this life. And he is the betrayer. I don't know which it is, but I pray he's not the one who will turn on me. All I can do is keep watch and remain ready to defend myself with my fire.

It's the most powerful magic I have, but I have no doubt it would work against him if I needed to use it—as long as I make certain he doesn't sneak up on me.

I hate that I have to be wary of him, when everything inside me wants to melt into his arms. Finding him is like finding another piece of my heart because this man is part of Bryndon. The one I pledged myself to. I gave myself to him: mind, body, heart and soul. To deny this pull I feel toward him is tearing at the very fabric of my being.

How cruel is it to be reunited with my beloved, and yet be afraid that the man I love is the one who will hurt me?

We were connected. Our lifeforce threads intertwined the moment he sealed me to him in our past life that day in the forest.

My soul remembers that connection and the bond that we forged. To be so close, but unable to touch him without fear, is a torture I never imagined.

Tears sting my eyes as memories of our life replay in my mind. "Please," I whisper under my breath. "Please, do not be the one who would hurt me."

CHAPTER 9

DAVIN

She still doesn't trust me, but I don't blame her. I was spying on her for months. Learning all her secrets and everything about her without her knowledge. She feels betrayed and violated because of it.

Clenching my jaw, I curse myself again for doing it. I knew it was wrong, but I couldn't stop myself. I became obsessed with her, and my obsession may be my undoing. The reason she will never choose me over Cael and Aris.

My heart clenches as I think of her in their arms. I always felt that she should be mine, and now that I know she was... I cannot bear to think of her with them.

Cautiously, I move closer to her bed. She lies on her back, her lovely golden hair spread out beneath her like a beautiful halo, her long lashes fanned over soft pink cheeks and her lips partially open in a small, round *o*. She is the most beautiful woman I have ever beheld. She is mine, and I am hers. I know this truth deep in the very core of my being.

Closing my eyes, I remember the day I sealed her to me.

She came to me in the woods and told me about the men who were supposed to become her harem. I could not stand it. I couldn't bear the thought of another man touching her. I made love to her like a man possessed, binding her to me: mind, body, heart and soul. At that moment, I cared not that it was wrong and that I was her guard and had no right to even touch her.

All I could think of was her in the arms of those other men and it drove me mad. Even now, I want only to seal her to me again—to make her mine in this life as she was in our last.

A deep ache centers in my chest as I think on Cael and Aris. Why is she theirs? Why have I been cursed to be reborn again only to never have her?

Even as I think this, I already know what I must do. If she is not destined to be mine in this life, I vow to always watch over and protect her if she'll let me. I want only to be by her side. Even if she cannot be mine, I will be her shield and her sword. Always.

CHAPTER 10

DAVIN

As the early morning rays of the sun filter in through the trees, Kyra appears so peaceful that I am loath to wake her. But I must. We have to keep moving. I don't know if the Dark Mages or the Guardians of Destruction are still searching for us, but I suspect that they are.

I'd like to believe they've given up, but I doubt they would. Kyra is important to them. This much I remember. They need her because she alone can wield the power of the elemental gemstones.

I remembered the stones last night as she lay sleeping. I saw them on the screen when she returned the first time to her apartment. Only two of them were in the crown. I wonder if she even knows where the others are?

"Kyra." I speak her name softly to wake her, but she does not respond.

"Kyra," I say louder.

Her eyes snap open, and she jerks up, raising her hands as

if ready to conjure her fire to defend herself. When her gaze meets mine, I hate that instead of relief I still recognize the same wariness she's had since we arrived here.

"It's morning," I offer. "We should continue on. See if we can find one of the towns."

"You're right. We need to find a Light Mage Guild. They can help us. They've helped me before when I was here with Cael and Aris."

I tip my head to the side to regard her. "You came to this part of the kingdom last time you were here?"

"No, but the two provinces I went to... I learned much from the High Mages." She pauses, and it is easy to read that she wants to say more but holds back for some reason. Probably because she still does not trust me.

"I remember the gemstones," I tell her. "You only had two in the crown. I saw them on the cameras. Do you know where the others are? Are you searching for them? Is that why you have returned to this world?"

She narrows her eyes. "You were the one with cameras everywhere. How do you not already know the answers to your questions?"

I deserve her anger, but I must find a way to gain her trust. If I cannot, I will be unable to fully protect her. "The cameras were damaged and I was unable to hear any audio."

She crosses her arms over her chest and levels an icy glare at me. "Well, at least I had some privacy then, didn't I?"

"Kyra, I only want to help you. Please," I plead. "Tell me what's going on."

When she doesn't answer, I drop to one knee before her. Bowing my head, I take her hand. "Please, my queen. I want only to protect you. To serve you and help you in any way that I can. My life is yours, now and forever."

Her hand trembles slightly in mine, and I lift my gaze to

find tears in her eyes. "I want to believe you, Davin," her voice quavers. "I do. But I don't know if I can trust you."

I stand. Without thinking, I cup her cheek. I'm surprised when she doesn't pull away from my touch, but instead leans into it. "I cannot take back what I did, Kyra. I should not have been spying on you. I—"

She shakes her head. "It's not just that, Davin."

"Then, what is it? Tell me, please. I need to understand."

A tear slips down her cheek as she steps back, pain evident behind her gaze. "We need to find the Light Mages. Only then, will I know if I can trust you."

"What does that mean?"

"Please, Davin. I cannot explain it all now."

I am desperate to understand, but I do not want to press her any further. If finding the Light Mages will help me to gain her trust, then that is what we will do. I turn my gaze out to the jungle. "We should go."

She nods. I'm surprised when she allows me to help her down from the web. She does not feel comfortable enough, however, to allow me to use my webbing to take us from tree to tree like we used to.

I am eager to find the Light Mage's Guild in this province. I want to do whatever it takes to earn her trust. In the meantime, I will do everything I can to show her that I mean her no harm.

It doesn't take long for us to find a trail through the jungle. A well-worn path used by horses and carriages.

"This must lead to a city."

"But which one?" she asks. "I wish I knew where we were."

A thought occurs to me, and I grin. "I may be able to find out."

"How?"

I look up at the trees. "I will climb up above the canopy

and see if I can visualize anything nearby. A landmark or a town or city."

She nods. "That might work."

"Wait here."

Before she can reply, I turn and shoot a web up to the tree, followed quickly by another as I ascend through the thick branches and leaves. When I finally break through the canopy, the sun is bright overhead as I gaze at the jungle all around us.

Butterflies take flight en masse from a tree nearby, coloring the sky in a brilliant display of green and purple as they flutter their delicate wings. Alora used to love these. They are much larger than the butterflies I've seen on Earth, but I remember them well. They are only found in this part of the kingdom.

I gaze off toward the north. A strange metallic reflection catches my eyes. As I turn to study it closer, I realize it is the golden spire of the High Mage's citadel in the distance. We are close to the capital city of Marisa.

Eager to share my news with Kyra, I quickly move back down the tree.

She stares up at me expectantly.

"We are close to the capital city and the High Mage's Guild."

"That's wonderful," she exclaims. "How far away is it?"

"It does not appear far, but looks can be deceiving. We would get there faster if you will allow me to carry you, my queen."

Her expression falls.

"Please, Kyra. I vow I will not harm you."

She lowers her eyes, her brow furrowed as if considering.

I pray she accepts my offer. The sooner we get there and speak with the mages, the better. She wants them to somehow validate that I mean her no harm—that she can trust me. Whatever they must do to prove that to her, I will eagerly offer myself up for.

After a moment she lifts her gaze back to me.

"All right."

My heart soars. All hope is not lost if she trusts me with this task. I cannot help the smile that lights my face. I turn my back to her, and she climbs on.

"Hold tightly, my queen."

CHAPTER 11

KYRA

As Davin swings from tree to tree with his webs, I wrap my arms and leg around him, clinging tightly to his form. With each movement, I can feel the flex of his muscles beneath me. My entire body hums in awareness of his. I remember this well.

His entire body is built of lean, solid muscle. Not an ounce of fat on him. I lean in just a bit and inhale his rich masculine scent. A hint of earth and spice.

He turns his head and flashes a handsome smile at me, and I can't help but give him an answering one in return. This is all so familiar.

"Shall I go faster?" He grins.

"Yes!"

He picks up the pace, shooting webbing from his fingers so fast we swing through the forest with dizzying speed.

Memories fill my mind, and I call out to him. "Faster, Bryndon!"

When we reach the edge of the city, he carefully drops

down onto a thick, low hanging branch. He reaches back and pulls me around to his front, onto his lap, keeping his arm wrapped securely around me so I won't fall.

"Look there," he whispers. "That vendor has clothing."

I sigh. This is the third time I've been transported here completely unprepared to blend in. I'm wondering now if when we get back to Earth, we should just remain clothed like the people in this kingdom just in case we get sent back here by surprise again.

People on Earth would probably just think we were cosplayers anyway.

I shift slightly to get a better look at the city and then still when I feel something harden beneath me.

I turn back to Davin, and he inhales sharply at my movement.

"Forgive me," he rasps.

Carefully, he lifts me off his lap and set me on the branch beside him.

Dropping my gaze to his pants, I note the large bulge beneath his clothing. His scent is stronger now for some reason. When I lift my eyes to meet his, his pupils are blown wide so that only a thin rim of violet is visible around the edges.

The heavy scent of spice surrounds me like a thick blanket. I breathe deeply of the heady mix and my heart begins to hammer as my pulse pounds between my thighs.

In the back of my mind, a memory returns. In his spider form, Bryndon used to emit a strong pheromone that I could never resist. Even as this thought surfaces, I find that I don't care. It always grew more potent with exertion. By the time he would finish taking us from one point to the next with his webbing, we could hardly keep our hands off one another. It was not on purpose. It was just an unintentional consequence of him taking this form—one I happened to enjoy immensely.

My entire body is humming with need and arousal as I stare deep into his eyes.

He watches me with a hungry gaze, his eyes full of desire and possession. Unable to stop myself, I lean in and press my lips to his.

His mouth is soft and warm, and his taste is incredible. I delve my tongue into his mouth, desperate for more.

His tongue curls around mine and a low moan escapes me as desire floods my veins. I wrap my arms around him and then crawl into his lap. I can't stop kissing him as I straddle his hips with my thighs.

He groans as I roll my hips against his. The friction between us is delicious, but it isn't enough. My mind is hazy with longing and desire. I dip my hands beneath his shirt, desperate to feel his bare skin against my own.

"I need you," I breathe into his mouth. "Now."

My words unleash something inside him, and he wraps his arms tightly around me, holding me close as he plunders my mouth.

His kisses are amazing, and I can't get enough.

"Davin," I whisper. "Touch me."

He cups his palm over my breast, teasing the soft peak into a hard beaded tip. I want him so much it is maddening.

"I want you, Bryndon. Please," I arch against him.

In the back of my mind, I know this is all happening fast, but I can't make myself stop. Something deep inside me craves his touch, and I want him so badly I can hardly stand it.

He stills and pulls back. His eyes search mine.

"Why did you stop?"

"My pheromones," he rasps. "That's what is affecting you. Not me." He pauses. "In this form... as the spider, you told me you always wanted me because of my scent. It was the pheromones, Kyra."

Even as he speaks, I can't stop touching him. My mind understands what he is saying, but my body wants other things.

"I want you, Kyra." He drops his forehead to mine. Panting heavily, he squeezes his eyes shut. "Gods, I want you so much, but not like this. I won't take advantage of the effect this form has on you, my queen."

I nod against him, unable to speak as I struggle to push down my desire.

He lifts his gaze to mine. "I love you, Alora. I love you still, but I… want you to want me when your mind is not clouded by this form, my beloved."

My heart is still hammering in my chest as I force myself to pull away. I open my mouth to speak, but he jumps from the branch to another one below us. Before I can ask what he's doing, he sends out a string of webbing to the vendor's stand.

The strings catch on several items of clothing while the vendor's head is turned, and Davin rips them back to us.

I gasp. "You shouldn't have done that! You could have been caught."

"I was careful." He grins and shrugs. "Besides, now we have clothes."

CHAPTER 12

DAVIN

As we change quickly, I have to force myself to look away from Kyra as she undresses. The taste of her mouth still lingers on my lips, and I long to kiss her again, but I want it to be when her mind is not clouded by my pheromones.

Inwardly, I curse myself. I should have remembered that my body produced these in this form. Alora used to love it, but Kyra... this is new to us in this life. Just because she wanted me before, does not mean it will be this way now. She already said as much.

Still, I have to try. I love her. I have to find a way to turn her from Cael and Aris—to convince her to love me again, like she used to.

I want her and it was so hard to pull away from her. With her body wrapped around mine and her lips pressed to my own, I could hardly stand to let her go. But I don't want her to do anything she might regret later.

We don't bother to bring our Earth clothes with us, leaving them in the tree.

Carefully, I lower us to the ground and we make our way from the jungle and into the city.

The medieval appearing town, with sandstone buildings and copper rooftops, is strange but familiar. I remember this area was prosperous, and it still seems to be. The cobbled streets are immaculately kept and lined with vibrant flowering plants and hedges. The windows of each building practically sparkle like new and everyone here is well-dressed in fine tunics and pants.

The light blue dress tunic and matching pants and shoes I retrieved for Kyra suit her well. They complement her lovely blue eyes. I am dressed in a deep blue tunic and pants. I chose this color because I remember couples in this area used wear the same color but different shades to indicate they were together.

Even if she has not agreed to be mine, I cannot help but want others to believe she is. I don't want other males to believe she is available.

She grins. "You did this on purpose, didn't you?"

I blink down at her. "What do you—"

She gestures to our clothing, and my brows shoot up toward my hairline. It's as if she has read my mind. "The matching blue clothing."

A smile tugs at my mouth. "And what if I did?"

She narrows her eyes, but I don't miss the slight quirk of her lips.

"Why do you always worry that I'll want someone else, Bryndon?"

My expression falls as the words leave her mouth. I lower my gaze.

"I cannot help it. Forgive me. I know you've already chosen Cael and Aris and—"

She presses a finger to my lips, silencing me as her blue eyes meet mine. "It's not what you think, Davin. I..." Her gaze darts all around us, as if worried someone may be listening. "I'll explain when we're alone, all right? I explain everything after we speak with the mages."

I nod even though I wonder what there is to explain. From what I saw on the camera, before I shut it off, it was all rather simple and plain as day for anyone to understand.

She has already taken Cael and Aris as her mates. She has chosen, and she did not choose me.

CHAPTER 13

KYRA

It's easy to read the sadness in Davin's eyes. He does not understand. He doesn't know that Cael and Aris and him... they're all part of Bryndon—the man he was before.

I want so much to comfort him, but I'm still uncertain. I worry that it might all be an act. That he may be just lying to gain my trust, hoping I'll lead him to the next gemstone. Hoping he can somehow turn me to the other side.

Astra said the way the Dark Mages turned Bryndon before was insidious. That he didn't even realize what they'd done to him until it was already too late.

I want so much to tell Davin everything, but I can't. Not until I know for sure that he is not the one who'll betray me.

It's so hard because he feels so familiar. The more time we spend together, the more I recognize Bryndon in him. Even though my mind is screaming that I should be cautious, my soul is calling out for his.

The threaded connection between us is there; I can feel it.

And yet, he is not just Bryndon. I recognize this. He is Davin as well. His life has been shaped by the experiences of both the past and this one.

As I study him, I can't help but be worried it could be him that will betray me. That's why I want to speak to the High Mage of this city. I want to know if they can read him like Aris was supposed to—to see if he is the one who will turn on me or not.

And yet, I worry that the mages may not be entirely trustworthy. High Mage Talwyn suggested the possibility that some of them may have been turned to the darkness. A small shudder runs through me as I remember the High Mage that tried to kill Cael.

I turn my gaze back to Davin. I don't want anything to happen to him. I know he can take care of himself, but I cannot help but worry anyway.

I'm also hopeful the mages may be able to return us to Earth. I miss Cael and Aris, and all of our familiars. I can only imagine how worried they are about me.

Tears swim at the edge of my vision, but I blink them back. I do not want to appear weak when we stand before the High Mage. I may be the Queen, but I have learned that I must earn their respect if I want them to follow me.

When we reach the entrance to the Light Mage's Guild, it's curious that the doors are not only open but there are no guards standing sentry.

Everything is silent and still as we slowly walk up the steps. My heart hammers in my chest when I realize the interior is dark. A cold breeze rushes past us, and a small shiver runs through me. Something is not right here.

Davin grips my forearm, stopping us abruptly. "I sense a... darkness here." He narrows his eyes. "Can you feel it as well?"

"Yes," I say under my breath. "We need to leave. Now."

Turning away from the building, we start down the steps.

The hairs rise on the back of my neck, but I dare not turn around. I already know we are being pursed.

A sharp pain stabs at my back. Warmth spreads out from the site as my limbs grow heavy and my vision begins to darken. I search my memory, and my mind recognizes the malishade poison of the dart. Closing my eyes, I fall away into the darkness that beckons me.

CHAPTER 14

KYRA

As my mind slowly awakens, the first thing I'm aware of is the dull pain across my entire body. It's as if my form is one large bruise—every muscle aching and sore. Opening my eyes, I see Davin tied up, lying beside me on the ground.

I try to move but my hands and feet are bound as well. Turning onto my back, I scan our surroundings.

It's dark, only a tiny sliver of light filtering in from the barred window high above our heads. Dark gray brick walls surround us and the floor is cold and damp. I don't know where we are, but it looks like a prison—three solid walls and one open one facing a hallway. I grasp a small stone on the floor and throw it toward the opening to test it.

It hits an invisible barrier, bouncing back toward me. Light arcs across the opening like fingering veins of lightning. It's an energy field. A magical one if we're where I think we are. As my memories slowly return, I think back on the

Light Mage's Guild in this province. We must be in the bowels of the building.

The open doors were a trap—a well-laid one that we were too slow to recognize and escape.

Sighing heavily, I curse myself. How could I not have recognized it sooner?

I roll onto my side and move closer to Davin. "Davin?"

His eyes snap open, full of anger. He tries to move, and then growls in frustration when he realizes his hands and legs are bound. He writhes against his bindings.

"Don't worry, Kyra. We're going to get out of here, my queen. My vow."

"How?"

He gives me a handsome grin full of mischief a moment before someone's voice calls out.

"You are awake."

I turn toward the sound and watch as a Mage in light gray robes steps through the invisible barrier. With long red hair, streaked through with white, and pale blue eyes, she studies us with a piercing gaze. The energy field shimmers around her a moment as she passes through.

She places a small tray of food on the ground and then kneels before me, flashing a thin-lipped smile.

"I had hoped you would come here. It was a gamble, you know? Once you took out our Guardian of Destruction in the jungle, we anticipated you might seek out the Guild, but we couldn't be sure. I am glad to see I was right."

"Who are you?" I grind out.

"I am High Mage Hyleah."

"What do you want?"

She stands and gives me an imperious look. "What all of us want who follow the one true God. He who brings about Destruction. We want you to join us."

"Never," I seethe.

Her eyes dart to Davin. "Perhaps you can be persuaded to change your mind. You care for this one, do you not?" Her nostrils flare. "You reek of his scent."

I start to wonder how she knows this, but when dark fangs extend on either side of her mouth and her eyes turn obsidian black, I realize she is like Davin. Able to take the form of a spider.

My mouth drifts open as her skin turns purple and her fangs drip with thick droplets of yellow venom. "We will feed you and make sure he remains unharmed in exchange for—"

She stops as I raise my bound hands, struggling to conjure a flame that never comes.

An evil laugh escapes her as ice fills my veins. "You cannot do magic here, *my queen*," she says mockingly. "Did you think we did not anticipate your power when we brought you to this cell?" She gives me a mock pitying look. "Your magic will not work in this place."

"But this will," Davin says.

I jerk my head toward him as he releases several strings of webbing from the tips of his fingers toward the Dark Mage, wrapping them tightly around her in a cocoon. She drops to the floor like a stone. With her mouth covered she can neither speak nor cry out for help.

He partially shifts into his spider form, and I watch as his canines extend into sharp, pointed tips. He bites at his bindings on his hands, shredding them. Then he unties his feet.

Davin rushes toward her as she begins chewing through her bindings as well. He drops to his knees and I watch in horror as he rips the fangs from her mouth and throws them on the floor.

She lets out a shrill screech, but it's cut off as he spins more threads around her, covering her mouth. Red blooms from her lips across the silken binding, spreading out as she writhes on the floor. Her eyes are full of rage as they meet mine, promising death if she can break free.

He rushes toward me and frees me from my restraints.

I rub my wrist. They're raw from the tightened rope that had been lashed around them.

The High Mage growls as she watches us, and I realize that I cannot leave her alive. If I do, she'll hunt us down the moment she breaks free. If she cannot turn me, she will kill us both.

I try again to conjure my fire but it will not work. I turn to Davin. "We cannot let her live."

His gaze hardens. "I agree."

He lifts his hands and shoots out a string of webbing toward the bars on the windows. "Stand back," he calls over his shoulder.

I watch in awe as he pulls on them until the mortar crumbles and the bars crash to the ground at his feet. He scales the walls and stands at the newly made opening.

When he turns back to me, he shoots webbing at our prisoner, securing it tight around her already cocooned form. His eyes meet mine. "Anything you want to ask her before—"

I shake my head. "I doubt she'd tell us anything anyway."

Without hesitation, he jerks her up toward the opening and over the side. It all happens so fast, my jaw drops as I stare up at him, impressed by his strength. I knew he was more powerful in this form, but I'd forgotten just how much so.

He looks over the wall, no doubt tracking her descent. I only know it's over when he jumps down and turns his back to me. He glances over his shoulder. "Climb on."

I quickly gather as much of the food as I can, and shove it into the two pockets of my dress tunic, and then climb onto his back.

As soon as I'm secure, he scales the wall to the opening. My eyes widen as I look to the ground. When I first woke up, I thought we were underground, but we're actually in one of the great spiraling towers.

The Mage's Guild sits at the very edge of the city. The jungle canopy spreads out below us as we stand precariously on the ledge. It's still dark, but the light of a promised dawn begins to spill over the horizon.

To the left, I can make out part of the city on the other side of the building. There doesn't seem to be any activity yet, and I'm glad. "We should be able to climb down the walls without being noticed," I tell Davin.

He nods. "Hold tight. It shouldn't take long to descend."

Using his webbing, he drops over the side and carefully begins to climb down the wall.

I try not to look down, but I can't help it. When I do, my stomach twists in a violent knot. I swallow against the bile rising in my throat as I squeeze my eyes shut.

"Try not to look down," Davin says too late. "I promise I won't drop you. We'll be all right, Kyra. I've got this."

Unable to speak I nod and cling even tighter to him, locking my legs around his waist and my arms around his neck.

The scrape of his body against the wall as he moves down the building, followed by several small bits of debris and rock as they fall loose and tumble to the ground is the only noise I can hear above the pounding of my heart.

I refuse to open my eyes, worried that I'll be temped to look down and make myself sick all over again. "Are we almost there," I whisper in his ear.

He stills, and I feel his neck twist as if to look down. He hesitates a moment before answering. "We're closer to the ground than we were before," he says teasingly.

"Now's not the time to tease me," I grumble.

His shoulders shake with soft laughter. "All right. I won't." He turns his head and presses a quick kiss to my arm. "I promise I won't drop you, Alora."

My heart clenches at just that small gesture. As if only now realizing what he's done, he sighs. "Forgive me, Kyra. Sometimes, I forget."

"It's all right," I tell him, my voice thick with emotion. "I do too."

"My dad and I used to go rock climbing when I was a teenager," he says. "This ability sure would have come in handy back then."

"Are you close to your parents?" I ask.

"They died in a transport accident right before I started college. Before I found Poe."

"I'm sorry," I whisper. "I lost my mom and sister not long ago as well. They were the only family I had left."

"Mine were too," he adds. "I was so wrapped up in my grief for a long time after they died. If not for Poe, I'd probably still be a mess."

"How long has she been with you?"

"About five years, give or take."

As I consider his answer, I realize it's the same for Cael and Aris. They all met their familiars around the same time, it seems.

"I really miss her," he adds. "I'll bet she's been worried out of her mind while I've been gone."

"I'm sure the others are looking out for her," I offer. "I know they did when Aris and I were here last time. Before they joined up with us."

It's easy to feel the tension in his body at the mere mention of Cael and Aris. As I consider our situation, I realize that if he was working for the God of Destruction, he could have so easily turned me over to the Dark Mages when we were caught.

He didn't, but part of me still hesitates to tell him too much. I'm worried it might be like it was for Bryndon. He may not even know his mind has been poisoned against me until it's too late.

Even so, my heart wants only to offer him comfort. To explain to him that I haven't forgotten the love that was between us before, and I have not betrayed it by taking two lovers.

As if sensing my hesitation, he sighs heavily. "I know you still do not trust me, and I don't blame you. I just... there is something I need to know."

"What is it?"

"Your... death," he says, the words thick on his tongue. "It was me, wasn't it? I was responsible somehow." He pauses. "I dream of you dying in my arms. I feel as if it was my fault, but I cannot remember why. It just... it doesn't make sense. I don't understand, and when I try to recall what happened, it's not there. My mind cannot access the memory.

"And yet, so many others are returning to me. It's as if this life is now blending with the memories of my old one. Even the way I think and speak is beginning to change." He shakes his head. "I need to know if it was me, Alora. Please. At least tell me this much."

Tears gather in the corners of my eyes. Emotions lodge in my throat but I somehow manage to speak around them. "You went to one of the Light Mages, asking for a way to protect me from the prophecy that foretold of my death. But the Mage betrayed you. He poisoned your mind and you did not realize it until it was too late. You had already —" the words catch in my throat as a tear slips down my cheek.

He goes completely still and then draws in a shaking breath. He reaches back and pulls me around to his front. I lock myself around him, and when I look into his eyes, they are bright with tears. "Forgive me, my queen," he breathes. "I —" his voice catches. "I do not deserve—"

"Don't say it, Davin." I drop my forehead to his as tears begin to fall. "I know it was not you. You were not yourself, Bryndon. It wasn't your fault."

His gaze is full of pain as it meets mine. "I understand now. You were right to choose Cael and Aris. I do not deserve you. I never did, my queen. I—"

He stills and his head jerks to look up.

"What is—" I start to ask, but stop as bits of rock and debris clatter down from above.

"Someone is coming," he whispers. His violet eyes search mine. "You need to hold tight."

Panic beats at my chest. "Why? What are you going to do?"

"We're going to have to jump."

CHAPTER 15

KYRA

Before I can say anything else, Davin pushes away from the wall.

A terrified scream erupts from my lungs as we fall with dizzying speed toward the ground. Several strands of webbing fly from his fingers toward the trees, halting our descent abruptly as he swings on one branch and then quickly catches another.

The jerking and sudden movements makes my stomach lurch. I barely manage to swallow back the bile threatening to rise in my throat as he moves through the forest and away from the city.

He moves so fast, the forest is a blur of purples and greens all around us.

"Are you all right?"

I open my mouth, but the words won't come. My heart is still hammering in my chest from the sudden fall, and I can hardly think beyond my fear.

"Can you see them?" he asks.

My arms and legs are wrapped so tightly around him, it's difficult to force myself to move when everything inside me wants me to cling to him even more. Somehow, I make myself peer over his shoulder.

Fast movement behind us catches my eye. It's a spider shifter like him, chasing us. Fear fills me as the glowing red eyes of the Dark Mage meet mine.

"Can you use your fire?" he asks.

"Yes." My voice is little more than a whisper as I lock my legs tighter around his waist and force myself to relinquish my hold around his neck.

"Don't drop me."

"I will not let you go. My vow," he replies, his voice full of conviction.

Raising my trembling arms, I call upon the magic that lies deep within me. Electricity arcs across the tips of my fingers as I conjure a blue orb of flame in each hand.

With a sharp flick of my wrists, I send them flying toward our pursuer.

He dodges them easily. A feral grin twists his mouth as his red eyes remain locked on mine.

Determination fills me as I quickly form two more. Taking careful aim, I send them spiraling toward him.

He cries out as one hits him in the side. Blue flames engulfs him, causing him to falter as he sends out a string of threads. Missing his mark, he slams into a tree.

"Did you get him?"

"Yes," I reply. My relief is short-lived. I watch in frustration as he quickly recovers and continues his pursuit. "But he's still following."

Anger fills me as I glare at our enemy. Closing my eyes, I grit my teeth as I concentrate and conjure every bit of magic inside me. A large, flaming blue orb forms, suspended between my hands.

Determined to end this, I tighten my legs around Davin and lift myself up just enough to allow me more movement of my arms. My heart pounds as I study the mage's movements to time my attack.

I will end this here and now. I will kill him and leave his charred and burning body in the jungle for his people to find. I want them to know what happens when they dare to attack their rightful queen.

I am a Guardian of the God of Creation. I am powerful even without the elemental gemstones. Today, I will remind them of that.

Drawing in a deep and stealing breath, I push the orb away, sending it flying toward the Dark Mage. I watch in satisfaction as it hits him squarely in the chest, enveloping his entire body in a brilliant burst of flame.

A feral cry of pain rips from his throat as he spirals toward the ground. He hits the forest floor and goes still.

"I got him, Davin!"

"I knew you could do it," he says, not bothering to slow his pace as he moves through the trees. "I'm going to try to put as much distance between us and the city as possible."

"Good idea," I reply.

As we continue through the forest, I'm struck again by how easily Davin could have turned on me if he'd wanted. He's had more than one chance to betray me, but he has not. My mind still urges caution, but my heart wants only to embrace him.

After what feels like forever, he finally stops. I'm still clinging to him as he balances on a too-thin-for-my-liking branch, and begins creating a web for us as he did last night. I notice he makes this one much larger, spanning five trees instead of three. As if reading my mind, he smiles down at me.

"We'll have earlier warning if someone steps on one of the threads."

"Good idea."

When he's finished, he lifts me into his arms. I'm too tired to argue that I can scale the webbing myself as carries me to one of the two beds he has made. Gently, he sets me down on the soft bedding of fibers. He gives me a warm smile as he spins a blanket for me and then gently tucks it over my shoulders. Just that extra bit of caring reminds me so much of our last life. Bryndon was always making certain that I was warm and never wanted for anything.

I remember the food in my pockets and sit up, offering him a piece of fruit and some cheese. "Here."

He shakes his head. "You keep it."

"There is enough for us both, Davin."

Reluctantly, he takes it from my hand. When we're finished eating, he turns his gaze out to the forest. "We need water. I will go find some for us. I believe there may be a stream nearby. Wait here."

I grab his hand. "No. Take me with you. I don't want to stay here alone."

Indecision plays out across his features before he finally nods. "All right."

Carefully, I climb onto his back. He sends a string of webbing from his fingers, and then begins to swing through the trees.

It doesn't make my stomach queasy anymore as we move through the forest in this way. I'm used to it after all the traveling we did today.

The sound of running water nearby draws my attention.

He drops down to the forest floor, and together we walk toward a small winding stream.

It's dark, and I can barely make out anything but the slight reflection of the moon across the water. Much of its light is blocked by the thick trees overhead. "Stay here," he whispers.

"Why?"

"I sense several creatures nearby."

Ice fills my veins. He said "creatures." As in more than one. I wish I could see as well as he can in the darkness as my mind conjures all sorts of terrifying images.

He turns back to me, gathering me in his arms. "I can scent your fear, Kyra. Please, do not be afraid. I vow that I will keep you safe, my queen. I merely did not wish for anything to startle you. So, I wanted to shoo them away before we approach the water. These creatures will not harm us."

"You're sure?" I ask, unable to hide the concern in my voice.

"Yes."

"How many of them can you see?"

He turns away, his gaze traveling over the darkened forest. "Only a dozen or so small animals." He pauses. "But they sense I am a predator and they are backing away."

I swallow against the knot of worry in my throat as he turns back to me. I notice his eyes are black instead of their normal violet color. Partially shifted as he is, I understand why they are moving away from us.

He is terrifyingly beautiful as he stares down at me. He lifts his open palm out for mine. My mind wars with my heart. I want to trust him so badly. Cautiously, I take his hand as my heart and soul win the battle that rages inside me.

If he'd wanted to harm me, he could have done so many times over already. I have to trust that if anything inside him was waiting to be triggered like it was in Bryndon, surely it would have happened when we were captured by the Dark Mages. It wouldn't make sense for them to not have used that advantage when they had us, or when they pursued us after we escaped.

He leads me to the water's edge. I drink several handfuls of water. I hadn't realized how thirsty I was. It's not quite cold, but it's not exactly warm either. I turn to him. "Do you think it would be safe to bathe?"

His eyes scan the area around us, and he nods. "I will keep watch while you are in the water. Then, I will go after you."

I shake my head. "I'm not going to allow modesty to put us in danger."

He frowns.

"We're both adults. Let's just hurry up and bathe together so we can get back to the safety of the web."

"You're sure?"

"Yes."

We turn our backs to each other as we strip out of our clothes. When we're finished, he keeps his gaze trained on the ground as he holds out his hand for me to take it.

When I do, he guides us to the water and we slowly walk in. It's cool and refreshing. I rinse out my clothes, and he does the same.

It's strange to be naked and so close to him like this. Instead of feeling vulnerable, however, need pulses through my veins. It would be so easy to go to him. To twine my arms around his neck and press my lips to his.

He turns to me. In his eyes I recognize the same desire that burns within me.

We remain that way for a moment. Each of us holding the other's gaze.

I force myself to lower my eyes. "We should get back."

He nods.

I put my bra and underwear back on, and he does the same with his boxers.

"We can lay our clothes out to dry on the webbing

tonight," he says as he bundles them up and then uses his webbing to secure them to his back like a makeshift pack.

Carefully, he lifts me into his arms to carry me back to the web. I wrap my legs around his waist and my arms around his neck.

He's so warm, I press myself against him as a cool breeze rushes through the forest. His heart beats a steady rhythm beneath my hand as I allow my palm to rest over his heavily muscled chest.

Even though we've bathed, his masculine scent is so enticing. Despite how strong his pheromones were earlier, I was too tired to give in to my wants as I did when we first reached the city. But now, desire flares inside me as need pools deep in my core.

His nostrils flare, and I know he can probably scent my arousal. If so, he does a good job ignoring it. At least, I think he does until I can feel something hard beneath me.

I swallow thickly. Neither of us say anything as he crawls back up the web. He carefully lays me down on one of the soft beds. "I'll keep watch while you rest, Kyra."

He stands and turns away to leave, but I wrap my hand around his forearm.

"Wait. Aren't you tired?"

He spins back to me. "I am fine."

Despite his words, it's easy to read the fatigue in his expression.

Heat flares my cheeks as his violet eyes stare intensely into mine. "Stay with me."

Hope fills his gaze. "Are you... certain?"

"Yes."

Carefully, he settles beside me, and I tug the blanket over us both.

CHAPTER 16

DAVIN

As she drapes the blanket over us, I lie as still as possible on my back. I'm too afraid to move, worried she might change her mind. The image of her staring up at me warily last night is burned into my memory, as is the knowledge that I am the one who took her life when we were Bryndon and Alora.

Tears fill my eyes, but I blink them back, staring up at the stars through the thick canopy of trees.

Her warm hand cups my cheek, turning my face toward her. Her blue eyes search mine. "What's wrong?"

With a slight clench of my jaw, I swallow against the lump in my throat as I barely manage to answer. "I can hardly bear it."

"What?" she asks.

"I am the one who took your life." Unable to help myself, I touch her face. "You are my heart. How could I have—"

She presses a finger to my lips, silencing me. "You did not

know what you were doing. Your mind was under the control of the Dark Mage when it happened."

I meet her eyes evenly as I sit up on my knees and then bow my head before her. "I vow that I will not fail you in this life as I did in the other. I offer my life and all that I am to you, my queen. I will watch over and protect you." I pause as emotions lodge in my throat. "I will be your guard and nothing more. As it should have been in our last life. I will help you find the rest of your harem and—"

She cups my chin, tilting my face up to hers. "You don't understand."

"What do I not understand, my queen?"

"Cael and Aris are not just part of my harem, they are part of you, Bryndon."

My brow furrows deeply. "What do you mean?"

"After I died... do you remember speaking with the God of Creation?"

I search my memories. Closing my eyes, I remember the day I went to her tomb. A bright light filled my vision and when I looked up, the God of Creation was standing before me. He placed a hand on my shoulder and gave me a pitying look. One I did not deserve.

I was the one who had killed my beloved. I had no right to mourn her as I did. I was not even worthy of having been hers.

My heart clenches as I stare deep into her luminous blue eyes. "I told him that I had bound you to me even though I knew it was wrong. I begged him to release you from—" my voice catches, but I somehow manage to continue. "I was never worthy of your love. I was your downfall. I had sworn to protect you, and I ended up destroying the one person I loved more than anything in this world."

A tear escapes my lashes but she quickly brushes it away

with the soft pad of her thumb. "You were always worthy of my love, Bryndon."

I shake my head. "No. I was no one. I was simply a guard. You were a queen. I knew it was wrong to seal you to me, but I… I wanted you so much. I could not bear the thought of any others even touching you." I pause as guilt fills me. "The day I took you from the prince when we came to this province… the first time I carried you through the trees in my spider form." I swallow hard and then force myself to speak the words. "I was so tempted to seal you to me that day. The way you looked at me as I bound you to the tree with my webbing. I pretended I was only teasing, but deep down, I knew if I had asked, you would not have said no. I could see it in your eyes. In my spider form, I appeared as a monster and still… you did not protest as my mouth hovered so closely to yours."

She touches my face, tracing her delicate fingers across my lower lip. "I wanted you that day as well, my love. Why do you carry guilt about this?"

"Because I knew it was wrong. You were not meant for me. You were supposed to take a harem. You were supposed to be surrounded by mates who would protect you." I pause. "But that day gave me hope. As wrong as it was, I allowed it to grow. I had already been in love with you before then, but my obsession grew even stronger after that moment."

"Why is that wrong?" she asks.

"Because I became the thing that I am now."

She frowns and I realize that I must explain. I must admit all of my sins to her and give her my truth, no matter how disturbing she may find it.

I continue. "I was not just your guard, I became your shadow. I was the darkness that watched your every move. Many times, I would slip into your room in the palace at night, watching you sleep. You were completely unaware that I was even there.

"I knew it was wrong, but I would watch you undress when you thought no one was looking. I observed from the shadows as you touched yourself, imagining that I was the one who made you release the soft cries of pleasure you made as you found your release."

She inhales sharply.

With a slight clench of my jaw, I meet her eyes evenly. "In this life, I've watched you through the window of your apartment when you thought you were alone, Kyra. The first time I saw you touch yourself... Afterward, I snuck inside while you were asleep and stole the bra and panties you were wearing when you did this. I keep them in a drawer in my desk."

She turns on her side and drapes her arm over my chest, resting her palm directly over my heart. It beats a frantic rhythm, and I draw in a shaking breath as everything about her calls to me.

Her blue eyes search mine. "You forget that you admitted all these things to me in our past life. And... I admitted my part in it too."

I frown. "Your... part?"

Softly biting her lower lip, she nods. "I knew you watched me. Why do you think I would leave the window open in the palace as I undressed?"

My heart pounds as she traces her delicate fingers across the muscles of my chest. "I touched myself, knowing you were watching, Bryndon."

A soft puff of air escapes me as need burns through me like fire. "You did?"

She nods. "And now that these memories are returning, I realize why you were spying on me in this life. It is what you did before. This is part of who you are."

Her warmth, her scent, her smile, her hair... all of these things draw me in, and I long so much to take her in my arms and seal her to me in this life as we did in the last.

With a slight clench of my jaw, I force myself to remain still. She is not mine in this life as she was before. Just because we were together then, does not mean she will choose me now. Even if she does not, I pray that she will allow me to remain as her guard, for I can think of nothing else I'd rather dedicate my life to than her.

"Davin?"

I turn to face her. "Yes?"

Her blue eyes search mine a moment before she cautiously reaches out to touch my cheek.

"You saved me."

Unable to stop myself, I lean into her touch. I smile at her.

"You saved me as well," I counter.

She smiles and my heart stutters.

"I'm sorry for how I treated you. I didn't trust you."

"No, Kyra. I am the one who should be sorry. Even if it was part of who I was... it was always wrong to have spied on you as I did. Both in this life and the last."

She presses a finger to my lips to silence me.

"You were simply doing what you used to do when you were Bryndon." A faint smile curls her lips. "It always made me feel so safe to know you were there... in the shadows. Always watching."

"I remember watching as you undressed. It always drove me half mad with desire."

She traces her hand down my arm and threads her fingers through mine. Slowly, she turns on her back, pulling me with her so that my hands are braced on either side of her shoulders as I stare down at her. She cups the back of my neck and pulls my head down to hers.

The warmth of her breath fans across my skin a moment before her lips brush against mine.

"I remember," she breathes and then presses a soft kiss to my mouth.

My heart pounds as she traces her tongue over the seam of my lips, asking for entrance.

When I open my mouth, her tongue finds mine and curls around it. Her mouth is soft and warm, and I cannot get enough of her taste.

My nostrils flare and I scent her arousal as her kisses become more urgent.

"Kyra," I pull back, my lips hovering above hers. I drop my forehead gently to her own and draw in a deep and steadying breath. "It's the pheromones. They're making you—"

"No." Her eyes meet mine. "It's not that. I want you."

It's difficult, but I force myself to push away. I lie down on my back and then wrap my arms around her, holding her close to my chest.

"You're with Cael and Aris. I don't want to do something you might regret later on, Kyra. I—"

"You don't understand, Davin. I love you."

"What do I not understand?" Frustration burns through me. "I know you're with them. You chose *them*. Not me. Why Cael and Aris? I have to know, Kyra. Why?"

She sits up and cups my cheek, turning my face to hers. Her blue eyes stare down at me full of sadness.

"I know it will be difficult for you to understand, but... they are you, my love."

I blink up at her, confused.

She cups my chin. "Cael and Aris are part of you, Bryndon. You do not remember, but the God of Creation told you that we would be reborn. You wanted to avoid the mistakes that led to my death. You begged him to force me to take a harem in our next life so that I would be protected." She pauses. "He granted your request, but not in the way you imagined."

"What do you mean?"

"You were reborn as five different men. Each of them is a part of you, Bryndon. That is who Cael and Aris are. They are you, and you are them."

CHAPTER 17

DAVIN

I search her eyes in confusion and find nothing but truth reflected back at me. As she speaks the words, the memory fills my mind. I remember the God of Creation agreeing to my request, but I did not know this was his answer.

"You are all different aspects of Bryndon," she explains. "But still, you are him."

Clenching my jaw, I struggle to push down the jealous possessiveness that rises inside me, even now as dawned understanding fills me.

"He was wise," I finally say. "The God of Creation knew it was the only way I would accept you taking a harem."

"But in splitting Bryndon into five men, one of them... one of you," she says pointedly, "still carries the darkness within him, planted there by the Dark Mage. I was warned by one of the High Mages of the Light that one of my guards will betray me in this life."

I search her eyes. "You thought it was me."

"Yes, but now—" She cups my cheeks. "I know it is not." She pauses. "If you wanted to harm me, you could have many times over by now. You could have sided with the Dark Mage back in the city and—"

"I would never harm you, Kyra."

Yet, even as these words escape my lips, the image of me stabbing Alora flashes through my mind. "You died in my arms." I brush the hair back from her face. "I was the one who betrayed you then. And now I... can't stand knowing that I did this, Kyra. I—"

She seals her mouth over mine in a fervent kiss, then climbs over me, straddling my hips with her thighs.

"It wasn't you," she breathes against my lips. "It wasn't you, Davin. Please, my love. You must forgive yourself."

In one fluid motion, I roll her beneath me, holding her wrists against the bedding with my hands as I pin her under my body.

"No, Kyra. We must stop. You don't want this. I was the one who betrayed you. You cannot forgive me for what I did. I do not deserve—"

She lifts her head, capturing my mouth in a passionate kiss, and gods help me, I can't pull away.

My control crumbles all around me, and I wrap her up in my arms. I pull her bra down, revealing the soft creamy mounds of her breasts. Capturing the left one with my mouth, I gently scrape my teeth over the soft peak until it hardens into a bead beneath my attentions.

She moans and arches up into me as she runs her fingers through my hair, holding me close.

Without thinking, I pull her hands away and secure them to the bedding with my web. I do the same with her ankles, leaving her open and spread out beneath me, unable to move.

Gasping when I realize what I've done, I lift my gaze, expecting to find fear in he expression. Instead, her eyes are full of desire and hunger that matches my own. I remember this well. This is something she loved about this form. The way I would tie her up and draw out her pleasure over several hours.

Her gaze holds mine as I slide my hands up her thighs. I dip my fingers into her warm, wet heat, and she moans as I tease at the sensitive pearl of flesh at the apex. She arches up into me. "More," she breathes.

I extend my nails into claws and tear away her bra and panties, leaving her completely bare beneath me. "You are perfect," I breathe as I stare down at her beautiful form.

I lean forward and press a series of small, suctioning kisses from her breasts down the length of her body. When I reach her mons, I look up and find her staring at me with a heated gaze. "Allow me to pleasure you, my queen."

She nods and I dip my head between her thighs. The scent of her arousal is more than I can bear, and when I drag my tongue through her folds, I groan as her taste floods my senses.

Her entire body quivers beneath my touch, as she struggles against the bonds that hold her. She gasps and whispers my name in a breathless sigh as I carefully insert two fingers into her core.

She is so soft, tight and warm, I can hardly stand it. My cock is hard and painfully erect with want to join our bodies as one. But first, I desire more than anything to mark her with my scent as we used to. Something about this form always stirred this need in me to cover her with my essence so that everyone would know she was mine.

But that was then. I do not know if she wants this now.

So, I push down my needs and focus on giving her pleasure.

"I want you, Davin," she breathes out. "All over me like you used to."

My head snaps up, and I meet her half-lidded gaze. "You're certain?" I rasp, barely able to hold back at the mere thought of her desiring this as much as me.

"Yes," she moans.

I drop my head back between her thighs, concentrating on the small bundle of nerves that make her light up with pleasure. She writhes beneath me and I band an arm over her hips to hold her in place. Her breath quickens and then her entire body goes taut a moment before she cries out my name as she finds her release.

Moving back up her body, I drag my cock between her folds. The warm, wet heat is such exquisite torture. I long to sheathe myself deep inside her, but she has not asked for this. She has asked for what we used to do, and that is what I will give her.

The tip of my cock bumps against her already sensitive bud of flesh between her thighs as I pump my fingers in and out of her channel.

Her head falls back, but I cup her chin, tipping her face back to me.

"I want to watch you as you come." I rasp, barely holding onto my control.

Nodding, her gaze never leaves mine as the small muscles of her channel quiver and flex around my fingers a moment before clamping down hard.

She cries out my name. Her release triggers my own and I roar above her as my essence erupts from my body, covering her with my seed.

Leaning down, I kiss her long and deep. She lifts her hands from the bedding and holds me close. I never used to bind her so that she could not escape, and I made sure to keep the webbing loose now as well.

I love that she trusts me enough, she not only allows me to bind her, she remains that way of her own accord while I pleasure her. She undoes the binding on her ankles and snuggles against me.

I weave a cocoon all around us, sheltering us from the cool breeze that drifts through the trees. When I'm finished, she uses my shoulder as a pillow and drapes her arm over my chest and one leg over mine.

I want more than anything to seal her to me, but she has not indicated she wishes to do that just yet. It is enough that she allows me to touch her like this.

My thoughts turn to Cael and Aris, and I release a heavy sigh. I know they're part of who I was, but it somehow does not make it any easier to think of them touching her.

This was my downfall—my intense possessiveness and jealousy. With a slight clench of my jaw, I force it back down. I will not succumb to my dark impulses in this life like I did in the last. If I want her to be safe, I have to accept that she needs a harem, just as she did in our past life.

As she lies nestled in my arms, I brush a stray lock of hair behind her ear and study her lovely face. She is just as beautiful in this life as she was in our last. I worry for her, though. We escaped the Guardian of Destruction and the Dark Mages, but she needs more protection than just me.

I know she can take care of herself, but her enemies are many. I saw it in Aris's mind. Although I did not recognize it then, it's returning to me now. Along with more information about why we have all been reborn.

"What are you thinking?" she asks softly.

"When Aris joined his mind to mine, I saw images. Disturbing pictures of what will happen to this world and Earth if we do not defeat the God of Destruction and his followers." I pause. "It's strange, but I did not remember them until now." I pause. "I also saw glimpses of what happened with them. How you recovered two of the gemstones. And even now, more memories of our past life return to me as well."

Her eyes meet mine. "It happened that way for Aris and Cael. Bits of memory and pieces of information slowly returned to them the longer they were here. Aris seemed to regain his memories faster, however, although I don't know why.

"It's the nature of what he is, I believe," I tell her. "His elemental power is Spirit, I assume, judging by how he used his mind to join with mine."

"It is," she confirms.

"And Cael's must be Fire," I add, remembering how I saw him conjure flame in his palm like she does.

"Yes."

"Mine is Earth."

Her small brow furrows. "How do you know?"

"Because I recall that I can do this." I close my eyes and concentrate all my energy on a nearby vine. After a moment, it begins to unfurl from the tree trunk, growing thicker as it snakes toward us. Several large fruits ripen on the ends. I remember how much she used to love these. They taste like strawberries, but much sweeter.

When I open my eyes, she stares gaping at me.

"That's amazing."

I look at her. "If I can do this, so can you. I remember that I was able to assist you with your powers but yours were by far much stronger than mine."

I take her hand and direct her attention back to the vine. "Focus, Kyra," I whisper.

She closes her eyes. Glowing green lights form over her palms and then spiral out toward the vine. I watch in wonder as it grows twice as fast as what I was able to get it to do.

She opens her eyes, and I smile at her.

"That was incredible. Your powers are so strong and yet,

they're not even at full strength." I pause. "Imagine how much stronger you'll be when we find the other gemstones."

She lowers her gaze. "Finding the other stones means finding the other guards as well—the two remaining ones."

A thought occurs to me. "I think I know who the fourth one is."

She gives me a curious look. "Who?"

"The detective." I swallow thickly, hating to admit again that I spied on him too. "I placed cameras in his office and home, hoping to follow any leads he had on your disappearance. He has a familiar—a serpent—just like we each do."

She looks at me. "I met Poe. While you were unconscious, she talked to us."

"What did you think?" I grin. "She's a bit snobbish, but I love that about her. She—"

"I'm afraid of spiders, Davin. And snakes."

My eyes snap to hers. "What?"

"I have a phobia."

I look down at my body. "But I... you've seen me transform and you didn't have a problem just now when we—"

She shakes her head. "That's different. You look more like a man with spider superpowers than a spider itself. But Poe... she may not look entirely like a spider either, but it's close enough that I'm definitely going to have to do something about my phobia before I meet her again."

I blink down at her. "I think if you spend time with her, you'll find she's more like a Victorian-era lady than a spider." I grin. "That should help."

I pluck a few of the fruits from the vine and hand them to her.

She stares down at the fruit. "At least we have food." Her expression sobers. "I don't know where to go, Davin. I thought the Mage's Guild would give us answers. Instead, it only made them follow our trail."

I hug her close. "We'll continue to the next city. In the meantime, we won't starve." I gesture to the fruit. "And we can hunt if you'd like meat."

She grimaces. "I'd rather try to locate some meat at the next city… something already prepared."

I lift my hand, waggling my fingers as I grin. "Leave it to me."

She smiles, but it fades quickly. "I hate stealing."

"I do too, but until we find some money or figure out how to make some, we don't have a choice."

I retrieve our clothing from the web, satisfied that it's now completely dry. "We should be dressed in case we have to leave quickly."

She nods. "You're right."

After we dress, nestles into me. "Let's get some sleep. We'll figure out what to do in the morning."

CHAPTER 18

DAVIN

My eyes snap open as movement vibrates along the threads of my web. I look at Kyra. She is still asleep. Quietly, I untangle myself from her arms, listening intently to the noises of the jungle to try to listen for whatever it is that approaches our position.

Carefully opening the cocoon, I peer out but see nothing.

I touch Kyra's shoulder and place a hand over her mouth so she will not startle and alert our pursuers that we are awake.

"Someone is here," I whisper. "They've disturbed the webbing."

She nods and then raises her hands, readying to conjure her fire at a moment's notice.

"I'm going to go out and see if I can find anything."

She grips my forearm firmly. "No. Don't go, Davin. Stay here."

My heart clenches at the concern in her eyes. "I'll be careful, my queen. I promise."

I press a tender kiss to her forehead, and then turn back to the opening in the cocoon. Quietly, I emerge, making sure not to disturb the long threads of the webbing as I move.

I move down the line where I detect the strongest vibrations and then still when I notice Aris and his peacock up ahead. I stand and raise my hand to call out to them, but something slams into me from behind, and we go tumbling across the webbing.

A low growl rumbles in my ear as strong arms wrap around me.

"Now, Aris!"

Aris lunges toward me and touches my shoulder. His mind joins with mine again, and my eyes roll up in the back of my head as I feel him filtering through my thoughts. He's searching to see if I am the betrayer.

I twist and writhe beneath their grasp, desperate to get away from the overwhelming sensation.

I know the moment he discovers that I am not the one who carries the darkness, because he immediately pulls away.

"It's not him," he tells Cael.

"Maybe not, but he had her underwear in his drawer," Cael grinds out. "We cannot trust him."

My head drops to my chest as my body goes limp. Whatever his mind link does, it drains all of my energy, and I can barely lift my head.

"I would never betray her," I groan.

"Davin!" Kyra's panicked voice calls out behind me. I look up to find her precariously walking across the threads toward me as fast as she can.

I shift my gaze to Cael, his eyes still full of fire as they look at me.

"You may not be the betrayer," he grinds out. "But you were spying on her for months."

"Stop it, Cael!" Kyra's snaps. "He wasn't spying on me, he was—"

"He had a pair of your panties and bra in his desk drawer," he grits through his teeth.

"I know," she says. "He already told me."

Cael gives her an incredulous look. "What?"

Aris stares at her with wide eyes. "He didn't just have them, Kyra. They carried his scent. He had—"

"Enough!" she tells them both.

Deep down, I know I should be ashamed, but I can't muster the energy to feel anything right now.

"I was obsessed," I offer by way of explanation because it's the best I can do right now in my weakened state.

"I'll say," Cael snarls. "But that ends now."

"No," Kyra says. "He's one of the guards. He's part of you, Bryndon. I love him."

She loves me. She truly loves me.

Happiness blooms in my chest.

"I love you too," I barely manage before I lose the battle to stay conscious. My eyes roll up in the back of my head, and I fall away into darkness.

CHAPTER 19

CAEL

My nails extend into sharpened claws, readying to rip Davin to shreds.

Kyra moves between us, shielding him with her body.

"No. He's one of the guards. He's part of you, Bryndon. I love him."

My heart stops. *She loves him?*

"I love you too," he murmurs. His eyes roll up in the back of his head and he goes still.

She cups his cheek, turning his face to her. "Davin?" she calls to him, worry evident in her tone.

Aris kneels beside her and takes her hand in his own. "I searched his mind. He's not the betrayer."

"I *know* that." She pulls her hand from him and levels an accusing glare at us both. You didn't have to hurt him."

"I'm sorry, my queen," Aris bows his head. "Forgive me, Kyra. I was only trying to—"

She turns to me. "Why did you lay a trap for him?"

I give her an incredulous look. "I thought he was trying to kill you." I gesture to the cocoon. "He had you in all that webbing, and I thought he was—"

"Do you not remember what we used to do when you took your spider form?"

Unbidden jealousy rises like bitter acid in my throat as I recall those days. Well.

With a slight clench of my jaw, I lower my gaze.

"Forgive me. We thought the worst. Especially when we found out how long he'd been watching you."

She stands and cups my cheek, her blue eyes staring deep into mine.

"He did this because he *is* you, Bryndon. Do you not remember how you used to watch me? You were my shadow." She pauses. "He was doing the same."

Aris sighs. "She's right." He gives me a knowing look. "We also had some of her clothing as well, remember?"

Her jaw drops as she stares between us both. "What did you have?"

I level an accusatory glare at Aris before I finally admit. "The slip you'd wear beneath your dress tunic. It—"

"Smelled of you," Aris finishes my sentence.

She takes my hand. "I understand you were worried for me. I didn't trust him either, at first. Especially after I saw the monitors in his apartment. But he saved me from a Guardian of Destruction and one of the Dark Mages." She stretches up on her toes and twines her arms around my neck before pressing a tender kiss to my lips. "I love him. He was you, Bryndon. Do you not see it?"

Reluctantly, I nod.

Her gaze drifts over my shoulder. "Where is—"

"Is it safe to come up now?" Lynx calls out from down below.

"Yes, you can all come up," I reply.

Kyra smiles as Lynx, Astra, Fin and Poe make their way toward us.

She kneels and embraces each of them, except Poe, warmly.

"I'm so glad to see all of you."

Lynx drops his head in her lap. "We were so worried about you, Kyra." He glances over his shoulder at Poe. "This creature kept insisting Davin would never harm you, but I didn't know if we could believe her or not."

Poe places her hands on her torso in a disapproving look. "Davin would never harm anyone."

"We see that now," Astra says.

"Yes," Fin adds. "Forgive us."

Poe crawls up the web and then onto Davin. She moves to his face and places her front leg on his chin.

"Oh, Davin. I missed you so."

It doesn't escape my notice that Kyra edges away from Poe and closer to me. I wrap a protective arm around her, tugging her close. It seems she might have a problem with spiders, and I can't deny that part of me is glad.

My nostrils flare, and I flick my eyes up to their cocoon nest. It seems they were doing what we used to do when I was Bryndon and took that form. The urge to drag Kyra away from here to make love to her is almost maddening in its intensity.

She hugs Aris and gives him a tender kiss. Even that sends a spike of jealousy through me.

I grit my teeth in frustration. I cannot, *should* not feel this way. It's wrong. Looking down at Davin, I sigh. He is as much Bryndon as I am, and I must accept and embrace him as I have Aris. I drop to my knees and gather him in my arms. Poe holds onto him for balance as I lift them both up.

"We need to go."

Kyra looks at me. "Where?"

Astra hands her the crown. "You must use it to find the next gemstone."

Kyra nods and settles it on her head.

"Now," Astra says. "You must concentrate. The crown will show you where the next one is located."

She closes her eyes, and after a moment, they snap open.

"The Great Pyramid. We must go to the Great Pyramid. It is there somewhere. I can feel it."

I turn to Aris. "Can you open a portal? Take us there?"

He shakes his head. "No. It would alert the Dark Mages. They would be able to track us."

"That must be what they did with Davin and me," Kyra interjects. "As soon as we got here, one of the Guardians of Destruction found us."

Aris's brow furrows. "This is indeed disturbing. It seems they're able to follow your light somehow. They're using it to track your movements when you use the portal. I remember now… they were known to do this to those they were hunting. It made transporting dangerous."

I recall this as well. I glance down at Davin and Poe.

"Regardless, we have to keep moving."

"Yes," Aris says, his gaze going distant. "I sense a gathering darkness behind us."

CHAPTER 20

DAVIN

wareness slowly trickles back into my mind and my eyes snap open to find Cael staring down at me.

"About time you woke up," he grumbles.

I look around me and see him, Aris, Kyra and all our familiars. We're still in the jungle, but no longer at my web.

I jerk up to sitting. Kyra rushes to my side.

"How are you feeling?"

I drop my head in my hand, rubbing at my forehead. I lift an accusatory glare to Aris, seated beside me. "Like someone was in my brain," I reply, unable to hide the bitterness in my tone.

"I'm sorry," Aris says. "I had to be sure you weren't the one who would betray her."

"If I was going to betray her, I wouldn't have bothered protecting her with my web, now would I?"

"How were we to know that's what you were doing?"

I roll my eyes. "Because it's what I did before—what *we* did before," I correct. "When we were Bryndon."

"So, you remember then," Aris says.

"Yes." I pause. "Not everything though. Not yet, anyway."

"It's the same for us," Cael adds. "Aris and I share some of the same memories but not all. It's as if—"

"Our memories are fractured between the five of us now," I finish.

They both nod.

Something alights on my forearm, and I look down to find Poe staring up at me, her expression full of concern.

"Are you well, Davin?" she asks. She narrows her eyes at Cael. "This brute insisted upon setting a trap for you even though I told him several times that you would not harm Kyra. You love her and you have ever since you first started…" Her voice trails off as if searching for the right words before finally settling on. "Observing her."

I smile at her. "He was just doing what I would have done. He was trying to protect her, Poe. Go easy on him."

"I'll try," She crosses her front arms over her chest. "but it won't be easy."

She turns her attention to Kyra, and I notice that my queen's eyes are wide as she stares down at my familiar. "Hello, Kyra," she says brightly. "I did not get the chance to tell you when we first met, but you are even lovelier up close than you are on camera."

I stop short of facepalming myself. Although I know Poe only means good, she keeps referencing how much time we spent spying on Kyra, and it's making me feel more and more like the stalker I kept trying to convince myself that I wasn't.

"Thank you," Kyra says. "You are… interesting. Davin has told me good things about you."

Astra settles beside Kyra, her green cat eyes studying Poe intensely. "Kyra is afraid of spiders."

Kyra's head snaps toward Astra. "Astra!" she admonishes.

"It is truth, is it not?"

Reluctantly, Kyra nods and it's easy to read the devastated expression on Poe's face.

"Oh," she says, taking a few steps back. "Forgive me. I will try my best to keep a distance from you."

Kyra reaches for her. "It's fine. I'll... get over it."

Lynx steps forward, his bright blue eyes searching mine. He darts a glance at Cael and then turns his attention back to me. "It seems you know everything about us, but we know... next to nothing about you. Other than that you are part of Bryndon, that is."

As he gives me a wary look, the fox is much different than when I watched him on the monitor. It seems he and Cael are of one mind when it comes to me, and it's going to take some time to gain their trust. And from the shared look they give one another, I may never earn their friendship.

"Yes, we know very little of you." Fin cocks his head to the side. "Tell us about yourself, if you will."

Aris runs a hand over the peacock's lovely blue-green feathered back, and in their eyes, instead of judgment, I note simply curiosity. Not the anger and mistrust that shines behind Cael and Lynx's.

Astra, on the other hand, stares at me as if she knows something I don't. And it unnerves me a bit. Her fluffy orange tail is curled tightly around her feet as she sits next to Kyra but her green eyes study me as if trying to stare into my soul.

"I..." I open my mouth to speak, but am unsure what to say. My life certainly isn't interesting.

"Where did you grow up in this life?" Fin asks.

"In Seattle. My parents died right before I started college." I close my eyes against the painful memory. "They were in a bad transport accident."

Kyra takes my hand, squeezing it gently as I continue. "They were wealthy and... everything passed to me. They left me more than enough to finish school, which I did, even though it was hard, but I—" I stop, as my voice catches. "It was... difficult," I finally finish. "But I got my degree and became a programmer. Poe found me about five years ago." She gives me a faint smile. "She's been my only family since then. She's my best friend and constant companion." I gently touch her foreleg. "I don't know what I'd do without her."

"I'm sorry you've been through so much," Aris says.

Kyra hugs me, and I'm surprised when she reaches for Poe as well, opening her palm and allowing her to walk onto it. She brings Poe close as she embraces me. Her eyes are bright with tears. "You and Poe not alone anymore, Davin." She glances at Cael and Aris and all their familiars. "You are family now."

Tears sting my eyes, but I manage to blink them back. "Thank you."

To my great shock, Cael wraps his arms around us both and then Aris does the same. When he pulls back, Cael nods.

"We were once one. You are now my brother and... I ask your forgiveness for the way I treated you at first. Kyra is right. You were only doing what Bryndon used to do. We were her constant shadow when we guarded her in our past life."

Fin looks at Cael. "Why did that go much smoother for Davin, and yet for Aris—the man you consider close to you as a brother—you nearly allowed him to wipe his memory of Kyra before you decided to stop him?"

"Fin!" Aris snaps. "That's in the past."

Fin tips his head up, ruffling his feathers. "I'm merely pointing out that Davin has been accepted much faster into the fold than you and I were. That's all."

Aris huffs out a laugh and pats his head. "You don't need to go starting stuff now, Fin. Everything is good."

Lynx lifts his paw and smacks the back of the peacock's head. "Yeah. Don't try to stir things up."

Fin puffs out his feathers. "Touch me again, Fox, and I'll peck at you."

Poe moves between them. Her form so much smaller than theirs.

"Excuse me," she says in her prim and proper voice. "But I believe it would be in all of our best interests if we were to work together as a unit instead of bickering amongst each other. I propose that—"

"First things first," Lynx interrupts. "*I'm* in charge of all the familiars."

Fin narrows his eyes. "Is that so?"

Astra chimes in. "We've already talked about this. You are not in charge. We are all equals."

"We all know foxes are the most cunning of all animals." Lynx sighs and then settles down on the webbing, folding his paws in front of him and appearing completely unaffected by their protests. "Don't worry, my leadership skills are impeccable."

Poe opens her mouth to protest, but I already know that once she begins, she'll launch into some long-winded, yet eloquent, speech that we don't have time for, so I interrupt.

"We should keep moving, don't you think?"

"He's right," Aris agrees. "Something still tracks us. It's far away now, but that can change quickly."

CHAPTER 21

KYRA

As we make our way through the jungle, I miss hanging onto Davin as he would swing from tree to tree with his webbing. It was so much faster and definitely much more exciting. I observe as he and Aris chat back and forth while Cael stays by my side, his brow furrowed deeply.

I reach for Cael's hand and thread my fingers through his. "What are you thinking, my love?"

He sighs. "I know he was Bryndon just like I was... and I know you need the others. But I feel like I was just getting used to Aris and now I'm thinking of the others we haven't even found yet." His eyes are full of pain as he looks at me. "I guess I'm just worried that your attention will be pulled in so many different directions there might not be time for—"

I wrap my arms around his neck and seal my mouth over his. He gathers me close, and I whisper against his lips as I cup his cheek. "I love you, Cael. Never doubt that. My love for you will not fade. Just as it never faded when you were Bryndon."

I lift my gaze to find Aris and Davin watching us. I motion them over and then pull them into the embrace as I meet each of their gazes. "Bryndon was my one true love. And I love each of you just as strongly as I did when you were him."

A noise behind us startles us and Cael turns a sharp gaze out to the jungle.

"What was that?"

He narrows his eyes and I notice Lynx do the same, his pointed fox ears turn in the direction of the sound as he stands beside Cael.

Lynx's eyes go wide as he jerks his head toward us. "A snake shifter. We have to go. Now!"

Alarm bursts through me as we break into a run.

"Take her!" Cael looks at Aris. "Fly her to safety while we deal with this."

Astra leaps into my arms and then disappears. She whispers in my mind, *We can fight too.*

Lynx, Fin and Poe each bond with Cael, Aris and Davin. Davin's eyes swirl black before returning to their normal violet hue.

Aris looks at me. "I know you can fight, but we need to save your strength for when we reach the pyramid. We don't know what we'll find there and we need you at full power."

Reluctantly, I nod, and he partially shifts into his peacock form and gathers me in his arms. His wings spread out behind him and then begin flapping furiously as we ascend toward the sky. We race up and over the trees as I watch below for Cael and Davin until they disappear from view.

CHAPTER 22

DAVIN

I glance down at my hands as a strange surge of power moves through me. I'm not sure what just happened. It's as if—

"*I'm here,*" Poe speaks in my mind. "*Inside you.*"

"What?"

"*We don't have time for me to explain. You just use your power. Can you feel it?*"

"Yes."

I turn to Cael, his eyes swirling blue and then green, and I realize that Lynx must be joined to him as well, just as Poe is to me.

"You ready?" Cael asks.

Not really, but I nod, anyway.

He turns his gaze back to the jungle, and we each take a defensive stance as something crashes through the vegetation, the sound growing louder as it approaches.

My heart thunders in my chest. Whatever this is, it is large and I worry we'll have a hard time taking it down.

A thick musky scent fills the air, reminding me of the terrible stench of a snake. A chill runs down my spine as I remember Lynx's words. He said this thing is a snake shifter, but for the life of me, I cannot remember what they look like.

When it finally emerges, I gasp as my gaze travels over its monstrous form.

With the upper body of a man and the tail of a snake, it is the naga of the ancient Earth myths made manifest before my eyes. Except, this monster is larger than any snake I've ever seen before.

He stops and studies us with a sinister gaze. His sharp, vertically slit pupils glow yellow as they rake over us like a predator sizing up its prey. His upper body is thick, broad and heavily muscled.

With short golden hair, a sharp nose and square jaw, I would think him typically human if not for the two sharp fangs on either side of his mouth, and the lower half of his form. He has a long, thick tail of shiny, interlocking golden scales that reflect brilliant beneath the light.

"Where is the queen?" he hisses. "Give her to me. Now!"

"Never," Cael growls. His partial fox form bristling with tension. He flattens his ears to his head and his tail whips agitatedly behind him as he holds his hands out before him, his nails now sharpened into lethal black claws similar to mine.

"She will be ours," he snarls. "We will take her and twist her until she bends to *his* will. She will serve the Guardian of Destruction and bring about the prophecy."

"What prophecy?" I ask.

He narrows his eyes. His long, forked tongue snakes out as if scenting the air as he bares two long fangs dripping with venom.

"The one that says the queen is destined to serve him. She

will be his before she regains the last gemstone. It is written and so it shall be."

"No it won't," I snap as I send several threads of webbing racing toward him.

He twists and writhes on the ground as they wrap around his form.

Cael leaps into his back, clawing and shredding skin and scales as the naga twists and slams against a nearby tree, struggling to shake him free.

Cael's eyes dart briefly to me and I understand in this moment what he is silently asking. He's the distraction so I can continue weaving my threads around its body to trap the large serpent.

As Cael tears into him with his claws, I shoot a series of threads from my fingers, toward the naga, wrapping them tightly around his form. Each time he twists or turns, I add another layer, anchoring them to the nearby trees until he's so covered that he can barely move.

He realizes too late that he is trapped.

Cael jumps off his back and runs over to me. His face split in a wide grin. "Good work."

As the naga writhes in his bindings, I can't deny that I feel oddly proud of myself in this moment and Cael's praise makes it even better.

He taps my shoulder. "We need to go."

"Wait!" I say.

I send another string of webbing toward him, making certain he is completely bound and unable to move. Even if he shifts forms back into a human, he should still be trapped.

"All right," I tell Cael. "Let's go."

As we race through the jungle, I search the skies for Kyra and Aris, but see nothing. I hope they are far from here. Even though the naga has been bound, I hate the idea of Kyra being anywhere near that monster.

As this thought crosses my mind, I think about the detective back on Earth. He had a snake familiar. If he is one of her other guards, that is his form—the naga. I remember now that, when I was Bryndon, I was able to take it as well. I only ever did so in defense of my queen. She did not like that form and neither did I. It was only out of necessity that I ever shifted to that sort of creature.

I feel sorry for the detective if he is, in fact, part of us. He got the worst of it, if this is truth. I fear Kyra will have trouble accepting him if this is what he is.

CHAPTER 23

ARIS

I hate having to leave my brothers behind, but I don't doubt that they can handle themselves. Kyra, however, is uncertain. Her worry beats at the back of my mind. I open myself completely to her, sending her a wave of love and calm to try to soothe her concerns.

"They are stronger than you give them credit for, Kyra. They will be fine."

"Thank you, Aris." Her mind whispers to mine through our connection.

As I scan the area around us, something catches my eye in the distance. I turn toward it. Whatever it is, it reflects the sun so brightly that it's almost blinding. I squint my eyes, trying to make it out better.

Kyra calls out, pointing toward it. "That's the Great Pyramid. It has to be."

She's right. I remember it now. The top of it is capped in gold to reflect the rays of the sun in honor of the Sun God.

He is Helios—the lover that was separated from Luna—Goddess of the moon.

"Aris!" Cael's voice calls out below us, and I swoop back down toward the trees. Gently, I alight in front of him, but I keep Kyra tucked close to my chest.

I look between him and Davin. "We found the Great Pyramid. It's not far from here."

"Good," Davin says. "Let's keep moving before something else comes for us."

"I will stay joined to you," Fin says in my mind. *"We don't know what awaits us, and you need your full power."*

"Thank you, my friend."

"We will all stay joined." Astra's voice filters through my thoughts as well. *"You will each need your strength."*

"You can all hear that, right?" Davin asks.

Kyra laughs. "You'll get used to it."

"This is lovely," Poe says in her chipper voice. *"All of us together in each other's minds like this. It brings back the memory of when Davin and I would watch you together on the camera as you all had dinner. I wanted so much to join you then and now—"*

"Thank you, Poe," Davin says, irritation lacing his words. *"I don't think they want to be constantly reminded that we were spying on them. All right?"*

"We were not spying, Davin," she gently chastises. *"We were observing."*

"Call it what you will, but it was—" Lynx grumbles.

"Stop," Kyra tells him, and he goes silent. *"We're not going to argue over this anymore."*

"Fine," the indignant fox replies. *"If you don't want me to mention that your new paramour is a creepy stalker, I will not speak of it anymore."*

Fin laughs, and I try my best not to.

CHAPTER 24

DAVIN

W hen we reach the pyramid, I am impressed by its size. It's similar to the great pyramids of Egypt but seems much larger. A series of steep steps leads up to a grand set of golden doors.

The entire structure is constructed of smooth, golden brown sandstone blocks. There are several symbols etched into the stone , but I am unable to read them or understand what they mean.

We make out way up the steps toward the entrance. Several small gardens line the various levels, surrounding all four sides of the pyramid. As we make our way up the steps toward the pyramid entrance, I marvel at the rich vegetation and brightly flowering plants.

It's as if these gardens have been kept up and remain separate from the rest of the surrounding jungle. Each level a wonder of various plants that I recognize come from other provinces, far from here.

"That's from Andara—the floating island province." Kyra points to a nearby plant, as if reading my thoughts. "And that"—she gestures to another—"is from the capital province of Valyra."

When we reach the entrance, I study by the heavy, gold metal doors. They are etched with an image of the Sun God and the Moon Goddess in a lover's embrace. Their story is so tragic; I remember it well.

They were in love, then forced apart. People used to honor them every year with the lover's chase. It is said that when he first saw her, he desired her and she him. He walked toward her, but she smiled and ran. He gave chase. For an entire year, he raced after her. When he finally caught up with her, he asked her why she was fleeing from him.

She told him it was because she wanted to know that he would always seek her out and never give up, no matter how difficult. They sealed themselves to each other in that moment and although they are now separated, he has never given up the chase for her.

Every morning, the sun rises, reaching for the moon as it sets.

Kyra runs her hands along a carving in the door. "The lover's chase," she murmurs, and I realize it is a scene of this story that she is referencing.

"Yes," I tell her, and her cheeks flush with warmth. "Do you remember when we would participate in this ritual?"

"I do." She smiles, softly biting her lower lip.

I chased her many times through the forest. When I'd finally catch up to her, I'd ravish her for hours on end.

Carefully, we push open the doors, and the moment we step inside, my eyes grow wide with wonder. I'd expected to find dark hallways and corridors. Instead, it's an oasis. A world of thick vegetation and sunlight unto itself.

"Where is this light coming from?" Aris asks, his eyes traveling over the space.

Tall trees and lush purple plants with vibrant red flowers fill the entire area. It's so large, it would be easy to become lost in this place.

"It must be some sort of magic," Cael whispers. "It seems much bigger in here than it should be, does it not?"

"He's right," Aris agrees. "I can sense it. Magic is tightly woven throughout this entire space."

The sound of running water draws my attention and I turn toward it to find a huge waterfall spilling down from the rockface above and into a great pool of sparkling clear water below it.

A light mist of steam rises above the surface and it looks so inviting. As we walk further in, the soft scent of delicious nectar of some sort fills my nostrils. A golden haze surrounds us, and I glance down at our feet, noting that with each step onto the purple moss beneath us, it releases this strange golden pollen into the air.

I breathe deeply of it and so do Cael and Aris.

"What is that?" Cael asks. "It smells wonderful."

Arousal builds deep within me as I inhale deeply of this scent. "It's intoxicating," I add. My cock grows so hard it's almost painful with the need to release. I swallow thickly as I turn to Kyra. Panting heavily, I long more than anything to sheathe myself in her warm, wet heat.

Cale and Aris turn to her as well. They stare at her with a lust-filled gaze. She looks back at us through heavy-lidded eyes.

"This place," Cael whispers, his pupils blown wide as his gaze travels over her form. "It is wonderful."

"Yes," Aris agrees. "It is."

"I agree," I tell them as my feet unthinkingly carry me toward Kyra. I wrap my arms around her and run my fingers through her hair. I grip the long golden strands between my fingers, and tip her head up as I delve my tongue into her mouth, exploring and tasting her.

I cannot get enough and neither can she as she returns my kiss fervently.

CHAPTER 25

KYRA

As Davin kisses me long and deep, warm hands snake around my waist and tug at my dress, pulling it down and away from my shoulders, leaving my top half bare.

I recognize Aris's strong hands on my breasts a moment later as someone else pulls my clothing off the rest of the way. Cael trails his fingers down by body, between my thighs.

I gasp as he spreads my legs, then his tongue slicks through my folds as he kneels before me.

Our familiars are gone, but I don't know where they went or even where we are now. All I know and all I can feel are the warmth of my mates and their hands and mouths all over my body. They carry me to a large flat stone. In the back of my mind, I realize this is an altar. A place where lovers would come at the end of their chase to consummate their bond.

Gently, Aris lays me on the stone. Davin spins a web, securing my arms and legs to the surface as I lie spread out before them. Cael leans down and kisses me long and deep before he finally pulls away. He turns to Davin and I allow my gaze to travel down Davin's form for the first time.

Last night, I could not see him clearly, but I can see all of him now. His cock is hard and fully erect. Liquid beads on the end and then rolls down his long, thick shaft. Heat pools deep in my core as I imagine what he might feel like inside me.

He moves over my body, capturing my breast, he laves his tongue over the already hard tip. A low moan escapes me as I arch up against him, straining against my bindings.

"I want you," I breathe.

His violet eyes meet mine, full of desire as he settles between my spread thighs.

"I want to seal you to me, Kyra, as we did in our last life."

"Make me yours, my love, and you will be mine," I whisper.

He notches his crown at my entrance and then slowly pushes deep inside me. I gasp at the sensation of complete and utter fullness as he sheathes himself fully in my core.

Cael and Aris stand off to the side, stroking themselves as they watch us.

Davin begins to move in a slow and steady rhythm at first. Each movement stokes the flames of my desire, but it isn't enough.

"More," I command.

He wraps his arms tightly up under me and drops down low so that there's no space between our bodies as he pumps into me, quickening his pace.

Each deep stroke becomes longer, more forceful and deeper. It's so intense, I'm nearly there.

He captures my mouth in a claiming kiss as he thrusts deep inside me. The delicious friction between us is more than I can bear. I reach the edge and then fall off into blissful oblivion and pleasure, crying out his name as I find my release.

He groans out my name. Delicious warmth blooms in my core as his cock pulses deep inside me as his release erupts from his body, filling me with his seed. It feels as if it goes on forever. I barely have any time to recover before Cael moves over me.

He shreds my bindings, freeing only my legs.

His intense emerald gaze holds mine as he notches his cock at my entrance. I moan as he enters me in one solid thrust. He begins a fast and urgent rhythm, driving my desire to new heights.

His desire matches my own as we chase our release. My every nerve hums in awareness of his body over mine.

He growls, partially shifting as he moves over me. Everything is already sensitive now that I've come already, so it doesn't take me long before I'm coming again. Wave after wave of pleasure crashes through me. He roars above me, his cock pulsing deep within as he fills me with his seed.

When he pulls away, I only have a moment to miss him before Aris moves over me. He positions his cock at my entrance. The breath stutters from my lungs as he slowly enters me, his gaze never leaving mine as he seats himself deep in my channel.

I'm already so sensitive that the muscles of my core quiver and flex around his length. He takes me in long, languid strokes. The tips of his fingers tracing over my body as he worships me completely.

Everything is so sensitive I cannot hold back. I gaze up at him. "I'm going to come."

He kisses me long and deep as he continues to move over me.

It's more than I can bear. My entire body locks up and I cry out his name as I reach my climax. He continues to thrust into me as I ride wave after wave of intense pleasure. When he comes, it triggers another orgasm within me and stars explode behind my eyes as he fills me with his essence.

He leans down and kisses me with a passion that steals the breath from my lungs. When he pulls away, Cael rips away the bindings on my hands.

Before I even realize what he's doing, he lifts me up as Davin moves beneath me, his back lying flat on the stone. He stares up at me, eyes full of lust as Cael lowers me onto his fully erect cock.

I only have a moment to adjust when I feel Cael at my back entrance.

"Will you take us both, my Queen?" he whispers, kissing my neck and lightly nipping my ear.

"Yes," I barely manage, breathless with desire.

Carefully, he pushes into me until he's fully seated. Together, they move deep inside me. Aris is lying beside us. I reach out and stroke his length in rhythm with Cael and Davin's movements. It's almost too much. I've never felt so much pleasure before.

My body is thrumming with desire and need as they pump into me. It's almost too much and yet, in the same breath, not enough. It's as is my body hungers for their touch and the fullness of them inside me.

With a keening cry my release roars through me.

Aris's cock pulses in my hand and then warmth covers me as his essence erupts from his body onto mine. Cael and Davin thrust deep inside me and then still as their cocks begin pulsing as they fill me with their seed.

When I open my eyes, the golden haze of pollen is thick in the air. Cael lifts me into his arms and carries me to the pool of water beneath the falls. He walks us both in. The warmth of the water surrounds us and it feels so good, I stretch in his arms.

He takes advantage of my movement to lean down and close his mouth over my breast. I gasp and then arch up against him as he turns me so that I'm facing him. I wrap my legs around his waist as he presses me against the stone beneath the water's surface.

When he pushes into me, I moan. Threading my fingers through his hair, I pull his lips to mine.

"You're insatiable," I whisper against them.

He smiles. "I always want you."

Warm hands touch my shoulders and Cael spins me around so that his back is to the rock as Aris moves behind me.

"Will you take me?" he whispers and nibbles my ear.

"Yes."

He slowly and gently pushes into me. The dual sensation is overwhelmingly intense, and I come with a low, keening cry. Warmth fills me a moment later as they pulse deep within and when they pull away, Davin wraps his arms around me.

He slants his mouth over mine and gives me a claiming kiss as he enters me in one long thrust. I gasp at the sensation of fullness deep within as he pumps into me.

"Gods, Kyra," he whispers against my lips. "I cannot get enough of you."

I wrap my legs tight around him, digging my nails into his back as each thrust becomes harder and deeper. Pleasure sparks and then roars through me as he pumps into me. Warmth floods my channel as I tighten around him. He covers my mouth with his, swallowing my cries as he holds me to him and the warmth of his essence blooms deep within my core.

When he pulls back, we're both breathless and panting. He carries me out of the water and I'm surprised when he takes me back to the altar. He bends me forward, casting webbing over my wrists to hold me in place.

Cael moves behind me, nudging my thighs further apart as he notches his cock at my entrance. I look over my shoulder, and his pupils are still blown wide. I push back against him, desperate for him to fill me as a golden haze of pollen thickens the air around us.

I want him so much, it is intense desire unlike anything I've ever known. I want each of them. I want them to take me over and over again, and I don't want to stop. Ever.

As he sinks deep into me, I arch back into him, enjoying the deep stretch inside as he fills me. Aris and Davin move to my side, each of them stroking their lengths as they watch Cael take me on the altar to the sun god.

When I wake, I'm not sure how long it's been, but my three mates are around me, holding me close as we lie near the pool at the base of the waterfall. My inner thighs are sticky with their release and the delicious ache between my legs reminds me that we've made love so many times I've lost count.

A fluffy white fox face comes into view, and I lift my head to find Lynx staring down at me. My first inclination would normally be to cover myself, despite the fact that because he links with Cael he already knows everything about me. Surprisingly, however, I find that I don't mind. I reach up and pat his head.

"Hi, Lynx." I smile up at him.

Astra moves to his side. "You need to get up. All of you. This place it's—"

"Making you ravish each other over and over again," Poe finishes her sentence.

"We believe it may be the pollen," Fin adds.

I gaze up at the swirling golden haze around me and stare at it in wonder. Closing my eyes, I breathe deep of the delicious and intoxicating scent.

Strong hands wrap around my waist, and then I'm pulled atop Cael. He enters me in one deep thrust, holding my hips firmly in place as he grinds up into me.

I moan at the delicious sensation, only remembering our familiars are here when I see Lynx roll his eyes and lower his head. He turns around, as do the rest of them.

"You have to stop. This is a trap to keep you here—to prevent you from finding the gemstone."

I gasp at the wonderful feeling of fullness as Cael moves deep within me.

"Don't want to stop," Cael groans. "Feels too good."

"Of course, it does," Lynx snaps.

I cry out as my orgasm sweeps through me so intense as Cael's cock erupts deep within, filling me with his seed.

"At this rate," Lynx snaps. "You've all made love so many times I wouldn't be surprised if you're already carrying cubs. This pollen is supposed to make conception easier."

"Cubs." The word floats through my mind along with the word conception, as I struggle to understand what he means as Davin pulls me to him and then enters me. He bears me to the ground, and I tighten around him as we come together and he fills me with his essence.

"Yes, cubs," Lynx says. "You all have to snap out of it. Now."

"What are—" I start to ask what cubs are because for some reason, I can't seem to remember. But I stop as Aris takes me from Davin. My toes curl with pleasure as he enters me slowly.

I moan as his slow and steady rhythm begins to quicken.

I'm almost at the edge, my mind full of pleasure when I hear Lynx tell Astra.

"They're going to make cubs here for sure. Then we'll really have a lot on our hands."

Alarm rushes through me as his words sink in at the same time that Aris and I begin to come. A strange burst of panic and intense pleasure pulses through me as he fills me with his seed.

CHAPTER 26

DAVIN

The lust-filled fog begins to clear from my mind as I drink the strange concoction Lynx and Astra made for us. I don't know what it is or where they found it. I only know it tastes sweet and the more I drink, the more my thoughts begin to sharpen.

"What happened?" I ask as I study the golden haze floating all around us.

"It's love pollen," Lynx answers. "It is a potent aphrodisiac that couples use to improve the chances of conception."

My eyes snap to Kyra, snuggled in Cael's arms. Each of us somewhat dressed thanks to our familiars. It still must be affecting me because thoughts of tearing the dress from Kyra's body and taking her again on the altar fill my mind.

Cael must be thinking the same. Cupping cups her chin, he kisses her long and deep as he pulls her onto his lap. Lynx reaches his paw out and slaps the back of his head, startling him.

"Stop! You need to focus."

Cael gives him a dark glare. "She is mine."

Lynx rolls his eyes. "We all know that. She belongs to each of you and you to her, but right now you need to finish drinking your potion so you can begin thinking rationally again."

Aris pulls her into his arms. "I'll hold her while you finish your drink."

Reluctantly, Cael lets her go. My jaw drops however when Aris seals his mouth over hers and rolls her beneath him. She opens her thighs, and Fin slaps the back of Aris's head as well, startling them both.

Aris blinks several times as if coming back to himself. He moves off of Kyra and helps her up to sit beside him. He sighs. "That pollen is strong."

We each finish our drinks.

Poe climbs up my arm and gives me an expectant look. "Are you yourself again?"

"I think so."

"Good. We need to keep moving."

Even as she says this, I wonder at the Dark Mages and Guardians of Destruction who might follow us here. Would they be affected by the pollen as well? I hope so. It would help us make up for whatever time we've lost in this place.

As if sensing my question, Astra looks at me. "The Dark Mages and Guardians of Destruction will not follow us in here. They are waiting for us to come out, however."

My gaze shifts back to the entrance. It seems far away, but I know looks can be deceiving. I may have been in a daze, but I do remember it didn't take long to reach the altar or the waterfall.

"Where do we have to go?".

Astra points to a dark hallway. "That corridor leads to the upper levels."

Aris's brows shoot up toward his hairline. "There are more levels?"

She nods.

"Do they each have pollen?" Cael asks. "Because even though we've finished our drink, I still—" He stops, but we all know what he means to say because we feel it too.

Even now, I could make love to Kyra again, and never want to stop.

"Let's go," Lynx says, switching his tail back and forth in agitation as he leads us toward the dark corridor.

CHAPTER 27

KYRA

Davin takes my hand as we move down the long hallway. A memory flits through my mind of us coming to this province. We found a field of love flowers, their pollen floating above them on a gentle breeze. We lost a whole day in each other's arms, but that was our plan. We wanted a child.

I lament that we never had the chance to have one. Now that we've found each other again, I only worry about having one too soon. I'm concerned we would not be able to protect a child without all of the gemstones.

I drop my free hand to my lower abdomen, wondering if the pollen worked for us here. Part of me hopes that it did, while the other can't help but hope that it didn't.

I sigh. I realize that if the God of Creation blesses us with the child we did not have in our last life, I will accept the blessing gladly.

I can't see as well as Cael in the darkness, but I can visualize enough to know that this corridor seems endless.

"This is the work of magic," Aris says. "We're in a pyramid, yet this hallway is a never-ending straight line. It should not be so."

"He's right," I add and then tug on Davin's hand as I stop.

Everyone stops and turns to me. "This is a trap," I whisper in alarm.

Deep and booming laughter fills the space around us, echoing down the hall as a sinister voice whispers, "Clever girl."

Cael pulls me behind him as Aris and Davin surround me as well. Each of them crouched in a defensive stance.

"Who are you?"

Each of our familiars joins with us. The energy that flows through my body feels like fire as Astra's mind links to mine.

"I'd heard you figured it out last time you were here," he replies. "I am one of the fractured souls. But I am stronger than the rest. I have been here many years, feeding off the ones who have come to my web."

I gasp when I realize what he means. The couples who come here and lose themselves in the pollen.

A rush of wind surrounds us and everything goes dark a moment before light filters in. It's so dim I blink as if that will somehow help my eyes adjust quicker. I step closer to Davin and something crunches beneath my feet.

I look down and then gasp when I realize it's a human bone and it's not the only one. There are piles of bones and bodies in here. The dried and decaying husks of people drained by this creature when they came to the temple to worship.

"How dare you!" I grind out. "How dare you take the Temple of the Sun god and desecrate it like this."

He laughs, the sound ominous and sinister. Glowing red eyes blink at me in the darkness and the sound of something scraping against stone fills the air. In the dim light, the creature comes into full view.

My jaw drops as I stare up at the giant spider. This is no shifter. This is a creature—a fractured soul turned into a hideous and bloodthirsty monster.

"Bow before me, Queen, or watch your lovers fall one by one to my venom."

My eyes snap to Davin's. If this spider has venom like his, one bite can be fatal. I saw what Davin's venom did to the Guardian of Destruction, and I can't stand the thought of that happening to any of them.

I step out from between them.

"Don't you dare touch them!"

I raise my hands, conjuring a ball of flame between my palms. I grit my teeth, struggling to contain it as Cael does the same. Together, we send the fire straight toward the spider. It slams against his body in a brilliant display of light.

He screeches, but appears otherwise unfazed. A web shoots toward us.

I try to spin away, but realize I won't make it. Cael pushes me out of its path, taking the direct hit.

It wraps tightly around him. He drops to the floor like stone. Aris goes to help him, but the spider sends more webbing at him, trapping him as well.

Davin shoots his own threads from his fingers, but the spider easily tosses them away.

"You think you can defeat me with something I, myself, possess?" He shakes his head as his red eyes blaze with fury. "Pitiful guard."

I drop beside Aris and Cael, using the power of my fire to eat through the webbing. I'm able to control it without burning them, as Davin stands between me and our foe.

The spider laughs darkly. "What do you really believe that

will do? You free them for but a moment before I'll capture them again."

He shakes his head. "I should just end one of them right now to prove that I am willing to do whatever it takes to bring you to our side."

"I'll never join you," I grit through my teeth. "I'd sooner die first."

"As you wish," he hisses.

Without warning, he shoots out a web, and it wraps around Davin.

Panic tightens my chest as the spider moves over the three of them, knocking me away.

I watch as he extends his fangs. Their long sharp points dripping with thick, yellow venom.

He leans down to bite Davin.

"No!" I jump between them.

The fangs pierce my flesh and agonizing fire burns across my skin and deep into my muscles as the venom moves through me.

"No!" Davin's voice rings in my ear. "Kyra, no!"

Despite my pain, I spin toward the spider. Closing my eyes, I conjure the power of the earth. I focus on the lifeforce of the vines growing along the outside walls of the temple, calling them to me and bending them to my will.

The structure rumbles and quakes all around us as I concentrate all my magic on wielding my power to thicken and strengthen the vines. I pull them through the structure, crumbling sandstone into dust as they snake through the pyramid.

An explosion of rock and debris rains down from overhead as they break through. The spider spins, but too late.

I wrap the vines tightly around each of his legs so tight his chitinous black armor begins to crack under the pressure.

Throwing my hands apart, the vines jerk at his legs, tearing them from his body in one swift movement.

He writhes on the floor, leaking thick, viscous orange fluid from his injuries before falling still. I watch as the light fades from his eyes and then turn back to my mates.

All of them have kicked the webbing free of their arms and legs. Davin pulls me into his arms and combs his fingers through my hair as he stares down at me, his eyes full of tears.

"Kyra, no," he murmurs. "Oh, gods."

"Help her!" Cael snaps at him.

"There is no way to cure her of the venom," Aris says.

"Yes, there is," Astra's voice speaks in my mind.

"The waterfall," Lynx says urgently. *"The waters of this place have healing powers."*

"The gemstone," I speak weakly. "Where is it?"

Davin turns to the dead spider and something green glows between its front set of eyes. I hadn't noticed it before, but now that I see it, I recognize it immediately.

"Take it," I barely manage. "We can't leave without it."

Unable to stay awake any longer, I close my eyes and fall away into oblivion.

CHAPTER 28

KYRA

When I wake, we are back in our bed in the castle. My three guards surround me. Aris is beneath me, and Cael and Davin are on either side. Each of them with one arm or two around me. I snuggle into their warmth as I stretch.

"What happened?"

Davin's eyes meet mine, full of sadness. "We failed to protect you."

"Forgive us," Aris says.

"Please, Kyra," Cael adds.

I frown. "You didn't fail. You saved me. I was dying and now... I'm here."

"It was our fault you were injured in the first place," Davin says. "We should have—"

"Stop." I place a finger to his lips to silence him. "I don't blame you. Any of you."

Aris sits up, bringing me with him. "We decided something while you were asleep."

"What?"

His gaze darts between Cael and Davin. "We are not going back to Earth this time."

"What? Why not?" I ask, confused. "We have to find the other guards. What about—"

Astra, Fin, Lynx and Poe walk into the room.

I don't bother to cover up even though I'm barely clothed. They saw everything in the pyramid already, so I'm no longer as embarrassed as I would have been before.

Astra jumps onto the bed, her green eyes meeting mine. "Aris is going to pull the detective through."

"What?"

"Yes," Fin says. "We've decided it would be safer to bring him here instead of us returning to Earth to retrieve him."

I frown. "We're sure he's one of my guards?"

Lynx shrugs. "Only one way to find out."

"And what if we're wrong?" I scoff. "We could give the poor man a heart attack doing something like that. And for what?"

Lynx places his paw on my hand. "It is a good plan, Kyra. The protective spell over the castle will cast him out if he is your betrayer. Only those who mean you no harm can come here, remember?"

I nod.

"Please, Kyra." Davin takes my hand and gives me a pleading look. "You've already disappeared twice on me. I won't have you disappearing a third time. I cannot bear the thought of losing you again."

"Besides," Aris says. "I believe it would be wiser for us to remain here. Davin told us about the High Mage in Linzyra. He said their Guild now serve the God of Destruction."

Cael looks to me. "The people of Lunaria need their queen. They will look to you for guidance. All this time, the High Mages of each Province have been the ones ruling in your stead. You must reestablish your permanent rule. If you do not, the God of Destruction will continue to use your absence to try to gather as many as he can to his side."

Aris steps forward. "If the detective is one of your guards and we bring him here, it will be safer to bring him across than for us to go to him. You will also have more protection when we search for the next elemental gemstone."

"Each time you've been pulled to this world accidentally, your life has been in danger," Cael adds. "Please, Kyra. It's safer this way."

As my gaze sweeps over my three mates, I realize they are right. This is the safest way. It's a risk, because the detective may be a random unsuspecting person, but deep down inside… I somehow know that he is not.

"I felt something when I talked to him," I confess. "I do believe he is destined to be one of my guards." I look at Aris. "Is there a way to pull him through gently?"

He darts a glance at Astra. Each time we've come here, the experience has been jarring. Falling through darkness and then slamming to the ground. I don't want that for this man. Especially since he'll be pulled through here all alone.

Astra places her tiny paw on my arm. "We will try to make his transport smooth."

Dressing, we all stand before the mirror as Aris and Astra bow their heads in concentration.

Our image ripples and distorts a moment before the detective appears before us. His eyes widen with alarm.

"Kyra?" he blinks.

"Seth." I put up my hands. "Let me explain."

"What are you—"

His question is cut off as he disappears a moment before he is suddenly standing in the room. He stares gaping at us.

"What is going on? Where are we?" he asks.

Cael pulls me behind him. "Let me explain."

"You!" Seth grinds out. "Let. Her. Go."

Cael growls at him. "No. She is ours and—"

In a whirl of dust and wind, the detective shift into a monstrous form. My jaw drop as I stare up at him, my heart pounding with fear.

The upper half of his body is a man, but the lower half a giant snake. He whips out his tail and knocks everyone back except for me. He pulls me into his arms in a crushing grip as he bares his fangs at Cael, Aris and Davin. Thick, yellow venom dripping onto the floor before him.

They shift into their forms as well, growling their displeasure.

"Let. Her. Go." Cael snarls.

"Or we will end you." Davin's eyes are black with anger as he bares his fangs as well.

Aris raises his arms and sends a burst of light toward Seth.

Seth's eyes roll up in the back of his head as he drops to the ground. His arms still wrapped around me in a crushing grip, as if trying to protect me even as he himself is attacked.

"Stop it, Aris! Stop!"

Aris lowers his hands, and Seth goes still.

His body shifts back into his human form, completely naked. It seems that when he shifts, his naga form is too large for his clothing. They lie shredded in a pile beside him, on the floor.

I take his hand as I kneel next to him. I cup his face and turn his head toward me.

"Seth?"

His eyes snap open. "Forgive me, Alora," he barely manages. "Forgive me." His head falls back and he stills.

I look at Aris. "Will he be all right?"

Davin answers, pursing his lips. "He's going to have a terrible headache when he wakes up."

"What was that that you did?" I ask Aris.

He shakes his head, his gaze drops to his palm, studying it intently. "I don't know. I just… raised my hand to him and it happened. I searched his mind without touching him."

I glance down at Seth's unconscious form, carefully combing the hair back from his face as his eyes remain closed. "I'm so sorry, Seth," I whisper. "When you wake up, I promise this will all make sense."

To be Continued in "Ensnared by the Serpent's Gaze"

ABOUT ARIA WINTER

Thank you so much for reading this. I hope you enjoyed this story. If you enjoyed this book, please leave a review on Amazon and/or Goodreads. I would really appreciate it. Reviews are the lifeblood of Indie Authors.

I have great news! The next book in this RH Superhero Romance is already listed on Amazon. *Ensnared by the Serpent's Gaze*

For information about upcoming releases Like me on Facebook (www.facebook.com/ariawinterauthor) or sign up for upcoming release alerts at my website:

Ariawinter.com

Want more?
Cosmic Guardian Series

Charmed by the Fox's Heart
Seduced by the Peacock's Beauty
Protected by the Spider's Web
Ensnared by the Serpent's Gaze
Forged by the Dragon's Flame

Once Upon A Fairy Tale Romance Series

Taken by the Dragon: A Beauty and the Beast Retelling
Captivated by the Fae: A Cinderella Retelling
Rescued By The Merman: A Little Mermaid Retelling

Bound to the Elf Prince: A Snow White Retelling

Once Upon a Shifter Series
Ella and her Shifters
Snow White And Her Werewolves

Elemental Dragon Warriors Series

Claimed by the Fire Dragon Prince
Stolen by the Wind Dragon Prince
Rescued by the Water Dragon Prince
Healed by the Earth Dragon Prince
Chosen By The Fire Dragon Guard
Saved By The Wind Dragon Guard
Treasured By The Water Dragon Guard
Taken By The Earth Dragon Guard

ABOUT JADE WALTZ

Jade Waltz lives in Illinois with her husband, two sons, and her three crazy cats. She loves knitting, playing video games, and watching Esports. Jade's passions include the arts, green tea and mints — all while writing and teaching marching band drill in the fall.

Jade has always been an avid reader of the fantasy, paranormal and sci-fi genres and wanted to create worlds she always wanted to read.

She writes character driven romances within detailed universes, where happily-ever-afters happen for those who dare love the abnormal and the unknown. Their love may not be easy—but it is well worth it in the end.

Thank you for taking the time to read my book!
    Please take a moment to leave a review! <3
    Reviews are important for indie self-publishing authors and they help us grow.

Connect with me at:

Facebook Author Page: Jade Waltz
    Facebook Group: Jade Waltz Literary Alcove
    Twitter: @authorjadewaltz
    Instagram: @authorjadewaltz

Email: authorjadewaltz@gmail.com

<u>Project Universe Links:</u>

Found
Achieve
Develop

Bird of Prey
Scaled Heart

Failure

<u>Project: Adapt</u>
Found

A failed human prototype. That's all she is...

Born and raised as an experiment, Selena's life has been filled with torture, betrayal, and distrust... but one night changes everything.

Sold, attacked, and on the run, Selena is picked up by a colony ship. Struggling to find her place on this ship and trying to understand the draw she feels toward two alien males, her already uncertain life becomes downright unimaginable when she learns new life is growing inside her.

Terrified her captors will find her and take her and her children back to a life of horror and captivity, she must learn to trust her saviors, and herself.

With the help of her two mates, Selena will fight for her freedom—or die trying.

Found is the first book in a space fantasy alien romance series which will have the heroine travel through the galaxy, experiencing new things and meeting multiple aliens along the way.

Order NOW!

Other Series Cowritten w/ Aria Winter:

Elemental Dragon Warriors - Alien/Dragon Shifter Romance - MF

Claimed by the Fire Dragon Prince

We set out from Earth in search of a new world. I never thought it would end with us crashing on a planet full of dragon shifters.

When I'm taken from my people by a fierce Drakarian warrior, my first thought is of escape. Varus is the Prince of the Fire Clan. He claims the glowing pattern on his chest means that I'm his fated one—his Linaya.

I doubt he's going to just let me go. But what does it mean to be fated to a dragon?

Read Now!

<u>Once Upon A Shifter - Fantasy Shifter Fairy Tale Retelling Romance – RH</u>
    Ella and Her Shifters
    Snow White And Her Werewolves